# Saved by the Sheriff

Carol Preflatish

Mainstream Romance

## DEDICATION

To my readers, I hope this book brings you as much enjoyment reading it as it did for me to write it.
To my family, thanks for your support.

# Chapter 1

Jaime Wilson shifted in her soft cushioned chair as she listened to Charlotte Miller, editor of *Real Mystery Magazine,* during their weekly editorial meeting. She could never sit still during meetings and this one was no different.

"Before we end our meeting today, I have one more thing. As you all know, we have an Assistant Editor position open now. Each one of you that have applied for the job are equally qualified, which makes the final decision impossible. What I have decided to do is make my choice based upon your next feature article. Bring me a story that will knock my socks off and the job is yours. Thank you and good luck."

All the writers got up and started out of the room, mumbling to each other about their most recent assignment.

"Jaime," Gabrielle called.

Jaime waited at the door for her best friend. "What do you need, Gabby?" Gabrielle Santoro, of Oriental decent, rushed to catch up. Her long black wavy hair accentuated her dark eyes and ivory skin.

"What are you going to write for that job?" Gabby knew Jaime desperately wanted that Assistant Editor job and would do just about anything to get it.

The ladies walked down the hallway toward their office. Once inside the cubical filled room, they sat at Jaime's desk to continue their conversation. "I did some research online last night," she whispered so the others wouldn't hear. "I found something about a family that disappeared thirty years ago in a small town in Indiana. No one knows what happened to the family. I'm going to Indiana to see what I can find out."

"That doesn't sound like a story that will knock Charlotte's socks off."

"It will when I discover what really happened to that family. I'm flying to Indiana tomorrow to do some hands-on research. What to come?"

"To the middle of a cornfield in Indiana? I don't think so. I bet there's not even a Starbucks there." She motioned toward the familiar coffee cup sitting on Jaime's desk.

"Oh, Gabby. Of course they have Starbucks in Indiana. Come on. Go with me. It'll be fun," Jaime begged.

"Even if I wanted to, I can't. I have an interview scheduled with the city coroner tomorrow that took me weeks to get set up and another one with Detective Marsh at the NYPD. But, you have to promise to call me every night while you're gone." She got up to leave. "I want to hear all about those handsome farmers in Indiana."

Jaime opened her desk to gather her things for the trip. *Digital recorder, camera, notebooks, pencils. I think that's it.* She put everything inside her bag and then unplugged her laptop computer.

"Hi, Jaime. What's going on?"

*Jonathan.* She looked up over the wall of her cubical to see Jonathan Muir, the last person she wanted to talk with right now. "Hi, Jonathan. I'm just packing up my things so I can go do some research for a story." She packed her laptop into the case.

"What are you writing about?" He walked around the corner and sat on the corner of her desk.

"I'm not going to tell you. Just like you aren't going to tell me your idea since we're both competing for the assistant editor job."

Jonathan got up from the chair. "You might as well hang it up now because I'm getting that job."

"The only thing I'm going to hang up is on you the next time you drunk dial me at two in the morning because you think your cat hates you." Jaime got up and walked out of the room.

The next day, her plane landed in Louisville, Kentucky, the closest airport to Royal, Indiana. After an hour drive, she entered the small rural town. "Wow, there really isn't a Starbucks here," she said to herself, as she drove down Main Street. She looked at the page of her notebook where she had written some addresses. "County Library, 513 West 5th Street. Hmmm, wonder where that is."

When she spotted a gas station at the corner of the street, she pulled in for directions. Inside she found a young lady sitting behind the counter, her bright pink fingernails glowing like neon. The smoke from her cigarette curled upward toward the rifle hanging from the ceiling with a sign attached to it that read, *Raffle Tickets $1.00 each.*

"Can I help you?" The young woman looked up from the magazine she was reading.

"I'm looking for the County Library. Can you tell me where I can find it?" Jaime asked.

"Back down that way," she pointed. "Turn right at the next street and then left at the one after that. It's a big white house on the corner. There's a sign so you shouldn't miss it." The girl took a drag from her cigarette and blew smoke in the air.

"Thanks." Jaime left the store and headed back down the street. After two turns, she found the old two-story white house with a small sign in the yard, *County Library*.

She pushed the front door open and walked inside. The house smelled of dust and mildew and the old floors creaked with each of her steps. "Hello, anyone here?"

"Yes. Can I help you?" An older lady stepped out from a back room. The little lady with her gray hair pulled back in a bun and wire-rimmed glasses reminded Jaime of her first-grade teacher.

. "Yes. I am looking for Annie Sampson."

"Well, you found her. I'm the head librarian here." She looked over the top of her glasses at Jaime. "And you are?"

"Jaime Wilson, from *Real Mystery Magazine* in New York City. I spoke with you on the phone last week about the disappearance of the Murdock family."

"Miss Wilson, yes, I remember. I can't believe a big-time magazine from New York would be interested in our little mystery here in Royal," Miss Sampson chuckled.

"Mysteries like these are what my magazine is all about. I came to do a little research on the disappearance and was hoping you can direct me to some people that might be able to give me some information." She took out her pad and pen. "Oh, and please call me Jaime."

The door behind Jaime opened and a lady with two preschoolers walked in. She smiled at Jaime and the librarian and followed the children deeper into the library where Children's books could be seen on the shelves.

"All right, Jaime. In that case, you can call me Annie. The best place for you to start is with some reading. I suggest you read through our most recent county history book to get some basic information. Follow me and I'll show where the books are." Jaime followed Annie to an area of the house where the history books were located. A gentleman was sitting at the table looking through a stack of typed pages.

"Here's the book I was telling you about. If you want, I'll let you check it out while you're here, but if you want to buy a copy, this is the man you need to talk to." Annie pointed to the gentleman at the table.

The man looked up at Jaime and then to Annie. "What book is that?" he asked rising from his chair

"Sam, this is Jaime..."

"Wilson. Jaime Wilson." She stuck her hand out to shake his.

"She's here from New York City to write a magazine story about the disappearance of the Murdock family."

"Is that so?" he reached out to shake Jaime's hand.

"This is Sam Morgan. He's the president of the County Historical Society."

"It's nice to meet you, Mr. Morgan. I'm sure I'll want to talk to you before I leave town."

As soon as she'd finished their introductions, Annie was summoned back to the front desk. Jaime had barely heard the front door open. "Miss Wilson, I suggest you be very careful while you're here working on your story," Morgan warned.

"Why is that?"

"There could be people in town that don't want that legend brought back up." He sat back down at the table and picked up the papers he had been going through.

"I don't understand what you mean."

Annie walked back into the room. "Jaime, there's someone I want you to meet." She motioned toward the tall, stalwart man following behind her. "This is Benjamin Hunter. He's our county sheriff."

Behind her stood a handsome man dressed in jeans and a flannel shirt. Instead of a uniform, just a badge hung from his belt. He ran his fingers through his thick, sandy brown hair that perfectly matched his brown eyes and neatly trimmed mustache.

"This is Jaime Wilson from New York City. She's going to write about the Murdock family's disappearance for her magazine."

"Miss Wilson." He tipped his head and flashed her a big smile. "Welcome to Royal." He looked over at Morgan leaning against the table. "Sam, how ya doing?"

"Ben, you ought to walk Miss Wilson out to her car and send her on back to the city. Tell her there's no story to the Murdock disappearance," Morgan suggested.

"Actually, I do need to go," Jaime uttered. "It's been a long day. Annie, if you don't mind, I would like to take this history book with me to read tonight."

"Sure, just bring it back before you leave town."

"Sheriff, if you wouldn't mind Mr. Morgan's suggestion, I'd like for you to walk out with me," she said.

"I'd be happy to, ma'am. I just need to drop off my book here." He placed his book on the counter for Annie to check back in.

Moments later Ben opened the door for her and they stepped outside. Walking to her car, they met a lady with a little boy. "Hey there, Billy. How are you feeling today?" he asked.

"I'm just fine, Sheriff," the little boy answered and smiled from ear to ear.

"Go on inside, Billy," the lady instructed the boy. Once he was in the library, she turned to Ben. "He had his last therapy yesterday and the doctor said he should make a full recovery."

"That's wonderful to hear, Mary. You bring him by my office later this week and I'll take him for a ride in my car."

"Thank you. We really appreciate all the times you stopped by to visit with him. It just made his day each time."

"Mom, are you coming?" Billy called from the door.

"I better get to him. Thanks again." She quickly went inside to join her son.

"What was that all about?" Jaime asked.

"That's Billy Rogers. He was hit by a car while riding his bicycle this summer. They weren't sure he was going to make it at first. But, with a lot of physical therapy, he looks as good as new."

"And, you went to visit with him?"

"As often as I could. It was a hit and run and we couldn't find the driver at first. I felt personally responsible for getting the driver. It took a couple of weeks, but we found the guy and he's serving time in jail for it."

*Impressive*, she thought. *He's both dedicated and caring about people.*

"What's so special about the Murdock family?" she asked.

"Nothing. They're just a family that disappeared thirty years ago. Some folks just made a mystery out of a mole hill."

"A whole family disappearing? That's some mole hill."

"No, we just have regular size mole hills around here."

Jaime did her best to hold in a chuckle. They reached her car and she leaned against it. Reporter mode. "You seem pretty young to be a sheriff."

He laughed. "Yeah, I guess I am. They tell me I'm the youngest sheriff ever elected in the county. Now, let me ask you this. How does someone from New York find out about the Murdock family?"

"The magazine I write for publishes stories about real unsolved mysteries from all over the country. We're always looking for stories like the Murdock's. I found it when I was doing some online searching."

"I can't imagine anyone being interested in that story or that there would be enough to write about. I bet you just stumbled onto a bunch of message boards with people swapping spooky ghost stories around the campfire. Conspiracy junkies."

"Oh, I plan on doing some thorough research on the disappearance. As a matter of fact, I would like to schedule a time this week that I could interview you about it." She reached in to her rental car for her planner book and opened it to the current week, which was clear.

"I don't think I could be much help. I was too young to remember anything from back then."

*What is it with these people? No cooperation at all.* "Well then, would it be possible for me to look over police reports on their disappearance? You do still have it on file, don't you?"

"Under the law, I can't stop you. They're public record. Stop by the Sheriff's Department tomorrow and someone will help you."

Jaime looked up and down the street. "Is there a hotel around here?"

"There's one out at the interstate, but mostly truckers stay there and it's kinda noisy. There's some vacation cabins for rent down by the lake. They're pretty nice and it being mid-week, they probably have a vacancy."

"Where would I find these cabins?" she asked.

"Go back down the street here and turn right. Head out of town for a couple miles and you'll see signs for the State Recreation Area. Follow those signs and you'll find the cabins."

She got into her car and started the engine, but stopped when the sheriff knocked on her window. She lowered it.

"There's no place to eat open this time of the year out by the lake. You might want to stop by the restaurant at the corner to get some supper."

"Thanks. I'll see you tomorrow at your office." She headed down the street. *Nice looking guy. Kinda sweet, but still it's hard to get a read on him. I'll have to make sure I mention him to Gabby when I call.* Taking his advice, she pulled into the restaurant parking lot at the corner of the street. *Corner Café, how original*, she thought.

When she walked into the restaurant, she found it to be nothing out of the ordinary. Taking a seat at a table, the waitress immediately came over with a menu.

"Evening. Can I get you something to drink first?"

Jaime looked at the menu. "I need to place a take-out order. I'd like a grilled chicken salad with Ranch dressing and an iced tea. Oh, and do you have any pie?"

The waitress looked over at the counter and then back. "We have pecan, chocolate, and raisin pies."

"I'll take a piece of chocolate pie, too. Thanks." She handed the menu back to the young girl and watched her walk back to the kitchen with the order.

Jaime looked at the clock on the wall and saw it showed four-o'clock. The restaurant only had a few customers. A group of elderly ladies sat at the table next to the window each with a cup of coffee and a piece of pie in front of them. Next to the wall, four men spoke among themselves about the politics in the county. *This is pleasant. The fast pace of New York has not yet found Royal, Indiana.* She thought about walking down the street in Manhattan compared to walking down the street of Royal. *Less people, less noise, less pollution.*

"I thought you'd like a glass of tea while you're waiting for your food?" The waitress startling Jaime out of her daydream. "Oh, I'm sorry. I didn't mean to scare you."

"No, you didn't. I was just thinking, I guess." She saw the girl had a glass of tea in her hand already "Thank you. Yes, that would be great."

"You're not from around here, are you?" She sat the tea, straw, and spoon on the table.

"No. I'm a writer from New York. I'm going to spend some time here working on a story." Jaime tore open a yellow packet of artificial sweetener and poured the contents into the tea and stirred.

"What kind of story?" The waitress sat down in a chair at the table.

Jaime felt odd about discussing this with the waitress, whose nametag said Jenny, but with any luck, just maybe it would prove helpful. Maybe it'd be easier than trying to squeeze information out of the Sherriff.

"Well Jenny," She cleared her throat, "It's about the disappearance of the Murdock family that happened thirty years ago. Have you heard of it?"

"Who hasn't? It's a real legend around here. Everyone is fascinated by the story."

"Really? So far, no one wants to talk about it." She took a sip of tea.

"Jen," the cook from the kitchen called. "Folks' coffee is getting cold and your take-out order is up."

"Your food's ready. You can pay at the cash register. If you can't get anyone to talk to you about the Murdock's, let me know. I have a friend who can tell you how to get to their old home place."

"Thanks. I just might be in touch."

Outside, the brisk fall wind blew leaves around her. It looked like rain might be coming and Jaime wanted to hurry and find those cabins the sheriff had told her about. Before leaving town, she made one quick stop to pick up some snacks at the small grocery store she found near the restaurant.

At least the sheriff's directions were perfect. After driving past the entrance to the Bison Lake State Recreation Area, she found the cabins only a short distance away. The carved wooden sign by the road said *Buckhorn Cabins* and a sign in the office window showed *vacant*. Outside of her car, she pulled the collar of her jacket closely around her to keep the cold air out, and scurried into the office.

"Evening, can I help you?" the gentlemen at the desk asked.

"Yes, I need to rent a cabin," Jaime replied.

"We're the only ones who rent cabins around here, and we don't like competition," he laughed at his own "joke".

"I'm probably going to be staying several days, if that isn't a problem."

The gentleman started typing on his computer. "It shouldn't be during the week, but we only have one available if you stay through the weekend. Would you like me to reserve it for you?"

"No. I think I'll be finished by then." She took her credit card out.

"Finished? You don't look like a hunter and that's about all we get this time of the year during the week."

*Here we go again explaining what I am here for. Well, at least last time it got me somewhere.* "I'm a writer from New York, working on a story about the disappearance of the Murdock family several years ago."

"Really?" a female voice spoke from behind her.

Jaime turned around to see a middle-aged woman coming into the room. She walked behind the front desk where the man stood.

"Yes, it's a very interesting story," Jaime uttered, getting an idea. "After my magazine publishes the story, it could bring more tourists to the area and more business for people like you."

"A lot of people around here won't see it that way. Most won't want people coming in for things like that," the woman sneered.

Jaime handed the man her credit card and her business card with her name and work address on it. "But, you don't think that way, am I right?"

"We're not originally from around here," he acknowledged. "My wife and I bought these cabins and moved here from the city. More business is always good."

He finished entering her information into the computer and handed her the credit card back. "You'll be in cabin number six. Follow the road in front of the office here all the way back. It's the last cabin and right on the water, too."

She took the key from the gentleman. "Thanks. I'm looking forward to a good night's sleep."

"You'll have no problem there. It's real peaceful down next to the lake," his wife assured her.

"Thanks." Jaime walked back outside and to her surprise, found the sheriff, now in uniform, leaning against his patrol car. She always loved a man in uniform and this one was no exception. Tall and lean, and when she stepped closer, she could hear the squeak of his leather gun belt as he moved. The sound of moving leather always excited her.

"I hope you didn't change into that uniform on my account."

Ben looked down at himself and chuckled. "No ma'am. I have a County Counsel meeting tonight," he said in his deep voice. Or perhaps Jaime only thought it sounded deeper now that he was in uniform.

"What are you doing here?" she asked.

"Just wanted to make sure you found the place okay."

"As you can see, I did."

"So, which cabin did the Ferguson's give you?" he asked.

"Ferguson's? Oh, the couple inside." She held up the key. "I'm in number six down by the water."

"That's a good one," he commented. "Did you get something to eat?"

Jaime sensed he had more of a purpose being here than just checking to see if she found the cabins. She couldn't read his emotions as easily as other men she had dealt with in her work, like the serial killer she interviewed a few years ago. "I stopped by the restaurant in town to pick up something before coming out. I'd ask you to eat with me, but I'm afraid all I got was a salad. Not something that's easy to share."

"No, ma'am. I don't really have time for supper. I need to be getting back to town for that Counsel meeting, but thank you anyway." He opened his car door.

"What time should I stop by your office tomorrow for that interview?" she asked.

"What?"

"The interview tomorrow. You told me to stop by and I could look through the department's files on the Murdock disappearance, remember?"

"Right. I remember. Around one o'clock sound okay?" he suggested.

"One sounds fine."

He closed the door and started his car. Before leaving he rolled down the window. "The files you need are stored at the old courthouse. We'll have to drive over there to find at them."

"Okay. See you tomorrow."

As he drove away, he gave her a little wave. *Interesting man*, she thought to herself. Once in her car, she drove down the little gravel lane to the last cabin. A sign on the door showed, *SIX*.

Juggling the salad, her pie, and drink in her hands while opening the door to the cabin, she walked inside. "Wow, this is beautiful." It was a small one-bedroom cabin. Inside the kitchen, she dropped her provisions on a small table with two chairs.

Back outside, she brought in her luggage from the car and the few groceries she got at the store. On the counter, she saw a coffeemaker. *Thank goodness. I can't function in the morning without coffee.*

With everything unloaded from the car, she finally sat down at the table to eat. The sun had set, but enough light remained that she could see the calmness of the water through the window that overlooked the lake. The difference between the hustle of the city and slower pace of the country was evident today. The thing she noticed the most was the noise, or lack of it. The silence surrounded her. No traffic, no sirens, no voices. "I think I could get used to this."

After eating, she tossed her take-out container into the trash and boiled some water on the stove to make herself a cup of chamomile tea. Then, she sat on the couch in the living room and picked up her cell phone. Surprisingly, she had a full signal. She dialed Gabby's number.

"Gabby, it's Jaime."

"It's about time you called. I was beginning to think you got lost in a cornfield or something. How's Indiana?" she asked.

"Not bad. I'm in a very small town and it's kind of nice around here." She took a sip of her tea.

"No kidding. How's the research going?"

"Well, it's the first day and already I have been told that I should go home by one person and another said she knows someone who can tell me how to get to the family's home place. Then, there's this sheriff that I cannot figure out." She heard something outside and walked to the window. "Can you hear this?" she asked Gabby, holding her phone toward the ceiling.

"Nope. I don't hear anything."

"It's rain hitting the tin roof of the cabin. It sounds so neat."

"Cabin? Where are you staying?"

"I'm renting a cabin near a state park or lake or some place like that. I'm right on the water. You'd love it." Jaime sat back down on the couch.

"You said something about a sheriff. Tell me more."

"Sheriff Ben Hunter. He's difficult to read and shows up when you least expect it. Like tonight for instance. Okay, earlier he suggested I stay at this cabin, right? Then when I came out of the office after renting the cabin, there he was! He was parked right next to my car." She picked up the remote control and turned on the TV but muted the sound.

"Maybe he's stalking you," Gabby teased. "Seriously, is he good-looking?"

"He's pretty nice looking—tall, sort of sandy brown hair, and blue eyes. He told me he is the youngest sheriff elected in the county. I have an interviewed scheduled with him tomorrow for my article."

"Boy, you move fast."

"Gabby, it's strictly business. Everything I'm doing is for my article. That assistant editor position is as good as mine."

"You better be right. Jonathan has been going around telling everyone that his story will be the best the magazine has ever had. Oh, and he kept asking me all day if I had heard from you and wanted to know where you had gone."

"You didn't tell him anything, did you?"

"Of course not. But, he is snooping around and he's been spending a lot of time in the editor's office. I don't like how it looks."

"Thanks for the info. I better go. I have a history book to read before morning. I'll call again tomorrow. Keep me informed about Jonathan. Oh, I almost forget to tell you. You were right, there are no Starbucks here."

"Good thing I didn't come with you or you would have one crazy lady on your hands. I have to have my coffee or I don't function. Should I Fed Ex you some?"

"No, I'll just settle for the regular kind they have here in the cabin. I better go. I'll call you tomorrow. Bye." Jaime disconnected the call and turned the sound on the television up to listen to the news and weather while she unpacked in the bedroom.

She placed her suitcase on the beautiful bed that had a purple quilt as the bedspread. She opened the closet to hang up her clothes. The aroma of cedar floated out from the red wood that lined the walls inside the closet.

After unpacking, she took a shower and dressed in comfortable clothes. Back in the living room, she curled up on the couch, pulling the knitted afghan from the back over her legs and began reading the history book she had got from the library. It didn't take long before sleep began to get the best of her and she decided to turn in for the night.

# Chapter Two

The following morning, Jaime arrived at the library just as Annie Sampson unlocked the door to open for the day. "Good morning, Miss Sampson."

The librarian turned around to see who had called her name. "Oh, hello. Please, it's Annie, remember?"

"I remember. Annie, it is."

"What brings you here so early? I figured you would be sleeping in after your long day yesterday." Annie opened the door and stepped inside followed by Jaime.

She looked down at Jaime's coffee cup. "I don't allow food or drinks in the library, only in the kitchen."

"Oh, sorry." She took one last drink and then disposing of the cup in the trashcan by the door. "My flight yesterday wasn't really that long and I slept great last night. The sound of the rain hitting the roof made it a very relaxing evening." She helped Annie unload the books from the return box attached to the wall and carry them to the desk.

"Where are you staying?"

"In a cabin down by the lake."

"The Ferguson's cabins?" she asked, scanning each book and then putting them on a wheeled cart.

"Yes."

"Their cabins are beautiful. You're lucky they had a vacancy." Annie pushed the cart into the next room and then started turning on the lights in the other rooms as she walked by.

"Don't you have anyone to help you here?" Jaime asked, following her around like a little kid.

"The county library budget is small. It mainly goes for my salary, utility bills, and buying books and magazines. I can usually handle it. The only time I have problems is when we get a bunch of school kids, but their teachers are a big help." She lifted a large book off the cart and tried to put it on the top shelf.

"Let me do that for you." Jaime took the book from her and slid it between *The Encyclopedia of Aircraft* and *Jane's Aircraft Recognition Guide.*

After helping put the rest of the books on the shelves, the two ladies walked back to the front desk. Annie sat at the computer checking the email and Jaime looked over all the notices posted on the bulletin board on the wall next to the desk.

"Is this meeting tonight?" Jaime asked.

"What meeting, dear?"

"This says the Historical Society is having a meeting tonight and someone is speaking about the disappearance of the Murdock family." She took the flyer down and showed it to Annie.

"Yes, it's tonight at the local museum."

"You have a museum here?" Jaime asked.

"Yes, it's one street over on Fourth. It's not much yet. The Society is trying to raise funds to do some repairs on the building and materials for more exhibits." Annie got up when two ladies came in to the library. "Good morning, ladies. Joanie, the book you were asking about came in yesterday and it's on the shelf in the back."

"Thanks Annie," the lady replied, heading to the back of the library.

"The timing for this is perfect for me," Jaime continued. "I'll be at the meeting for sure. Will you be going?"

"I'll be there, but honey…" the old lady's voice crawled to a cryptic pace "be careful. This is a subject that people around here don't like outsiders digging in to."

"I don't understand. It's a fascinating story."

Annie began whispering. "Some folks believe that the family was killed and their bodies disposed of near their home in a ravine and that the person responsible is still living around here. They don't want things stirred up."

"If that's the case, why would the Historical Society have a speaker on the topic?"

"Because they need the money for their building. A lot of people come to the meetings when they talk about the Murdock's and they usually leave donations in a bucket while there."

"Well, I'm still going. I'd be crazy not to." More people started coming into the library now and Jaime felt she in the way. "I'll see you at the meeting tonight. I think I'll go get some breakfast."

Jaime headed out to her car and saw a police car parked behind it on the street. With dark windows, she couldn't see who sat inside, but she knew. *Sheriff Ben.*

The door opened, but it wasn't the sheriff getting out. Instead, another officer, a deputy sheriff, approached her. "Ma'am, is this your car?"

"Yes, I rented it at the Louisville airport yesterday."

"Were you aware that the taillight is broken?" he asked.

She walked to the rear of the car and saw the red plastic over the light was smashed. "How could that have happened?"

"Good question. You need to get that fixed right away. I doubt that light is working at all and that's a traffic violation. I could write you a ticket, you know."

*Damn small town cops.* "I understand. Is there some place in town I can get it fixed?"

"On the south edge of town is a garage that my brother owns. He could fix that for you in no time." The officer smiled.

"Thanks."

"Are you the lady who came here to find out what happened to the Murdock family?" he asked.

"Not exactly. I came here to write about the mystery, not necessarily to find out what happened, but if it turns out that I could, it would certainly help my article."

"Six-nineteen, Central Dispatch," the radio blared from the police car.

"Have a nice day, ma'am," the officer shouted as he got into his car and drove off.

Jaime started toward the side of the car to get in, but something caught her attention in the sunlight. On the ground under the broken taillight she could see tiny pieces of red plastic. She picked up a few of the pieces to examine them closer. Someone had broken her light while she was in the library and she had a suspicion that the deputy had something to do with it.

Back in her car, she drove to the south side of town looking for the garage owned by the deputy's brother. She had heard about small town speed traps, but never one that busted your light. Ahead of her on the right, she saw a sign, *Bob's Garage*.

"What an original name," she stated to herself. She checked her watch and it showed close to ten-thirty. Breakfast was going to have to wait until lunch. *I should have enough time to get this fixed, eat a bite, and make it to the interview with the sheriff by one.*

Immediately, a grease-covered young man walked out of the garage. "Howdy, can I help you?" The patch on his shirt said, Chris.

"Yes, Chris, my taillight is broken. Do you think you could fix it right away? I don't want to be late for an appointment."

"Let me take a look." He walked to the back of the car. Jaime got out and matched him step for step. "Yeah, I think I have a lens to fit that. Have a seat inside and I'll get right on it."

"Thank you so much." She reached in the car to retrieve her purse and then gave him the keys. "A deputy in town told me I needed to get it fixed or he would write me a ticket. It wouldn't surprise me if he was the one who broke it so I would come to his brother's garage to get it fixed. Or maybe he was trying to set us up on a date."

The mechanic laughed. "That would be Jerry, my brother."

She looked at the sign on the front of the building and then to the man's name patch. "But, your name is Chris and the sign says Bob's."

"Oh, I bought this place from Bob Hawkins. Folks around here don't like change, so I kept the name. Anything else you need done while you're here?" he asked.

Jaime closed her eyes and shook her head. "No, only a receipt so I can get reimbursed by the rental company for the repair. Thanks." She walked inside the building to the office area where she found a padded bench to sit and wait for her car.

Already sitting there was a middle-aged man reading the newspaper. He moved over a little to make more room for her, giving her a smile.

Above the door, a television was tuned to EPSN and showed highlights from the baseball playoffs. "Do you like baseball?" the gentleman asked her.

"Only if the Yankees are playing."

"Too bad they didn't make it this year." He folded the newspaper and placed it between them.

"May I?" she asked, nodding toward the paper.

"Go right ahead, I already know everything that is in it."

"You must have been waiting for a while to have read the whole paper."

"No. I'm the editor of the paper. That's today's issue and it's still fresh in my mind."

*The Editor. Finally, someone in my business.* "Hi, I'm Jaime Wilson, from New York. I'm here to do research for an article I'm writing about the disappearance of the Murdock family." She held out her hand to shake.

He took her hand and gave it a firm shake. She liked that. Handshakes always tell a lot about people and his told her he was honestly interested in meeting her.

"I've heard about you," he retorted.

"You have? I only arrived here yesterday."

"My name is Kenneth Morgan. I believe you met my brother, Sam at the library yesterday."

*Is everyone related around here?* She wondered. "Yes, I remember him. He's president of the Historical Society."

"That's him. How's your story coming along?"

"I'm still in the research stage. The sheriff is going to help me find the old files from his office about the disappearance and I'm going to go to the Historical Society meeting tonight. I understand an expert is going to be speaking there tonight about the Murdock's." She got up and helped herself to the free coffee.

A young man stuck his head in the office looking around. "Mr. Morgan, your car's ready. Chris said he'll send the bill to your office, if you want."

"That'll be fine, Jimmy. Thanks."

"I'll bring it around the front right now." He disappeared from the room as quickly as he had entered.

"If there's anything I can help you with, Miss Wilson, please don't hesitate to ask. I'm usually in the newspaper office all day."

"Do you keep an archive of your papers?" Jaime asked. "I noticed the library keeps the actual papers, but nothing is cataloged."

"Yes, I do. They're on microfilm and can be viewed at the office and all of the articles are cataloged."

"I'd love to take a look at them some time this week, if I could."

"Certainly, I'll tell the receptionist to expect you. Stop by anytime after today." He left the room and went out to his awaiting car.

"Miss Wilson, I have your light fixed." Chris told her when he walked into the office.

She sat her coffee down and walked over to the counter to take care of the bill. "How much do I owe you?"

He started writing on an invoice sheet and then pulled it off of the holder it was attached to. "Twenty-three dollars should take care of it."

"Do you take Visa?"

"Yes, ma'am. I do."

She handed him a credit card and he swiped it through the reader and returned it to her. Seconds later the receipt printed and she signed it.

"Thanks for your business."

"Thank you for repairing it so fast." She took the keys from him and hurried to the car. She would have just enough time to have a quick lunch and then meet with the sheriff.

It was eleven-thirty when she walked into the Corner Café for lunch. Surprisingly, they were not busy like she thought they would be. Jenny greeted her as soon as she stepped in.

"Hi, Jaime. Take a seat on this side of the restaurant and I'll be your server," Jenny exclaimed.

Jaime obliged and walked to a booth next to the window. As she passed the empty table next to her, she saw an issue of the *Messenger News*, the local newspaper, and picked it up since she hadn't had a chance to read it earlier. She scanned the paper while waiting for Jenny to come take her order.

It had the usual front-page news, county commissioner's meeting, a fire that destroyed a family's home, and a criminal trial where a child molester was convicted.

"How are you today?" Jenny sat down a glass of iced tea. "I remembered what you drank from last night. I hope that's what you wanted again."

"Yes, perfect. Thanks." She folded the newspaper and set it aside. "What's good today?"

Jenny handed her a menu. "Our special today is smoked sausage and cabbage with mashed potatoes."

Jaime thought that sounded good, but a little too heavy for a noon meal. She looked over the menu. "I think I'll have a grilled chicken salad with Ranch dressing again. Oh, and hold the onions." She didn't want to take a chance on offending the handsome sheriff later.

"Will do. I'll be right back."

Jaime picked up the newspaper again and opened it. On page three, she saw a picture of the sheriff standing next to a dead deer lying in the back of a pickup truck. Underneath the photo, it captioned that he had killed the deer on the opening day of hunting season and that it was the biggest one brought in. *I'll have to scan and email this to Gabrielle tonight. She'll get a kick out of seeing Sheriff Ben.*

Just as she finished reading the newspaper, Jenny brought the salad for Jaime. "Would you like some more tea?" she asked.

"No, thank you. I'm fine." She unrolled the silverware from the napkin and then placed it on her lap. "Jenny, the other night you told me you knew someone who could tell me where the Murdock family had lived."

"Sure. My cousin, Bobby James, could tell you right where it is. That's him over there is the blue shirt." She motioned over to a group of men eating on the smoking side of the restaurant.

"If you get a chance, could you ask him about it? But, please don't let anyone else hear you, okay?

"Sure thing." Jenny headed back to the kitchen while Jaime started eating.

She looked at the clock on the wall and saw she still had plenty of time before her appointment. At that moment, she heard the bells on the door ding and saw the sheriff walk in.

His brown uniform showed off his lean, but muscular physique. Now that he was out of uniform, she discovered just how much she liked his body. He removed his hat and scanned the room, finally looking her way. He smiled and walked over when he saw her.

"Afternoon."

"Good afternoon to you. Are we still on for our meeting in..." she looked at her watch. "Forty-five minutes?"

"I'll be there."

"Would you care to join me?" she asked.

"Oh, ah, no. I can't. I just came in to pick up an order of food for my deputies and me. Thank you, though. I appreciate the invitation. Maybe another time before you have to go back to New York."

He almost looked embarrassed to say no. "Absolutely. It's a date. I mean I'd like that. Maybe we can discuss the Murdock family, for my article."

"Sheriff, your order's ready," Jenny called from the counter.

"I'll see you in about an hour." He stood and walked away.

"Sheriff?"

He stopped and looked back.

"I forgot to ask, where your office is located?"

He looked out the window. "See that big building over there?" He bent down with his arm extended over her right shoulder pointing out the window. She hadn't been this close to him before and the scent of his cologne took her mind off his pointing. "That's the courthouse. Go inside the front doors and the Sheriff's Department is straight ahead."

"What?" She exhaled, clearing her head. "Oh, okay, straight through those doors. Right, got it. Thanks."

He went to the counter for his order and she returned her attention to her salad, still enjoying the scent that lingered around her.

"He's a handsome man, isn't he?" Jenny's voice snapped Jaime out of her daydream.

"What? Who?"

"The sheriff. He's a handsome man." She refilled Jaime's tea glass from a pitcher.

"I suppose so. Thanks." She took a drink.

"He's single, too."

"Really?" Jaime cleared her throat.

"Jen, you wanted to see me?" Bobby James approached.

"Yeah. This lady wants to know where the Murdock family lived," she whispered. "She's writing a story for a big magazine about their disappearance."

"Yes, please sit down," Jaime motioned toward the seat.

Bobby sat across from her in the booth and Jenny made him scoot over so she could sit, too.

"So, can you give me directions?" she asked

"If you ain't from around here, you'd never be able to find the place, even with perfect directions. It's out in the middle of no where."

"Could you take me there?" she quietly asked.

"I don't know. The family that owns the property now doesn't want anyone nosing around out there. They've called the cops on artifact hunters before."

"Artifact hunters?"

"The area where the Murdock family lived and where it's suspected they were killed is near some rock shelters at a federal geographical area. Indians lived in those shelters and people are all the time looking for arrowheads."

"I really need to see the place and maybe take some pictures. I'd be willing to pay you for it," she offered.

Bobby looked around the restaurant. "If I take you, we would have to hike in from the back way. It's a long walk, if you think you're up for it."

"Just tell me when and where to be."

"Why don't you meet her here tomorrow morning?" Jenny suggested.

"This would be a good place to meet since I really don't know where many other places are," Jaime mentioned.

"Okay. I don't have to be in to work until noon tomorrow, so how about we meet here at seven in the morning?"

"I'll be here." She reached across the table and shook his hand.

"Wear shoes that you can walk a long distance in."

A worried feeling suddenly came across her. "How long of a hike are you talking about?"

"It's about a two-miles."

She slowly shook her head up and down. "O...kay. I'll be here in the morning."

Bobby got up and joined his buddies at the counter to pay their bill.

"Don't worry, Jaime. It's supposed to be a beautiful day. Perfect for a hike. I'll make up some sandwiches and coffee to take with you tomorrow," Jenny assured her.

Jaime finished her salad and wondered where she could find a store to purchase some hiking boots. After using the restroom and paying her bill, she left for her meeting with the sheriff.

Just as he had showed her, the County Judicial Complex was about four blocks away from the restaurant and it took only a matter of seconds to reach it. Before getting out of the car, Jaime touched up her lipstick. Satisfied that she looked okay, she went inside the courthouse.

Sure enough, once through the metal detector, right in front was the Sheriff's Department. Several people mulled around in the hallway and walked in and out of some of the offices. She walked up to window where a female officer sat.

"Can I help you?" the officer asked.

"My name is Jaime Wilson and I have an appointment with Sheriff Hunter."

"I'll let him know you're here."

Jaime stepped back while the officer picked up the phone.

A few minutes later, Sheriff Ben stepped out from a door and in his deep baritone voice, he uttered, "Miss Wilson, please come in."

"Thank you, and please call me, Jaime. I hope you don't mind me coming a little early."

"Not at all. Right this way." They walked down a hallway past a few rooms and finally to his office in the back. She took a seat in the small office and he sat behind his desk. "I looked for the files on the disappearance of the family and like I thought, they are still in storage at the old courthouse. We'll need to drive over there."

"Okay. I can follow you in my car."

"There's no need for that. I'd be glad to drive us," he suggested.

She paused for a moment deciding whether she should ride with him or not. *What could it hurt?* "Let's go then." She picked up her laptop bag that she brought with her.

The sheriff led her out the back door to his police car.

The drive to the old courthouse took only ten minutes. Jaime expected the building to be old, dark, and dingy, but she was surprised when she saw the building they had parked next to was a fairly modern brick building. The year, 1965, was carved into the cornerstone of the building in front.

"When did the offices move out of this building?" she asked.

"About five years ago, I think. I wasn't living here at the time."

He unlocked the side door where they parked, flipped on the light switch and walked in first. The floors were tiled and Jaime's shoes squeaked with each step as she followed. They walked around one corner and the sheriff stopped next to the old County Clerk's office.

"The records are in the vault," he said, opening the door. "Wait while I go in here to get them."

Jaime shuddered at the eerie quiet inside the building. She could hear the sheriff rattling the vault door and then the creek of it opening. *This would make a great haunted house in the dark*, she thought. From where she stood, she could see across the hallway through the glass windows of the doors to the courtroom. The rows of pews were still there and she imagined what proceedings went on in there over the years.

"Here you go."

"What! Oh, you scared me," she exclaimed. The sheriff put a dusty box on the counter.

"Sorry. I didn't mean to. This is the box of files about the Murdock's. We can sit at the table over there and go through them."

She walked around the counter to the table. "I need to plug in my laptop and scanner to make copies."

"There's an outlet back here," he motioned toward the wall on the far side of the table.

She took a tissue out of her bag and dusted off a chair and then the table. "It looks like it's been a while since anyone worked here."

"No one comes here unless they are doing some family history research and then someone from the Auditor's office has to come with them."

"I'm surprised to see that the utilities are still on here."

"The County is using the old courthouse as their archive of the county records. A constant temperature has to be maintained in order to preserve those records," Ben explained.

"I think it's great that your local government is making the effort to preserve the history of the records." Jaime started setting up her laptop and attached her scanner so she could copy some of the documents.

"Would you like something to drink?" he asked.

"You have beverages here, Sheriff?"

"There's a drink machine down the hall that the Historical Society keeps stocked for those people that are doing the genealogy research. It brings them in a little money."

"I'll take a diet drink, Sheriff."

"You know, it looks like we're going to be working on this together for a while, please call me Ben."

"Okay, Ben."

While he was gone to get the sodas, Jaime began looking through the files piled on the desk. "*Achoo.*" The dust caused her to sneeze. She thought back to the reason for her being here. Could she really write a story good enough to earn her that editor job? And, the sheriff, she wondered how much help he could be, or will he end up being more of a distraction than an aide.

"What took you so long?"

"I heard some noises and I needed to check on it." He handed her a can of diet soda.

She popped it open and took a drink. "I really needed this. It's so dry and dusty in here. I thought I was going to choke." She laughed and started typing something on her laptop.

"So what did you read on the Internet that made you want to come all the way down here and write about our little mystery?"

"I found an article written by a former resident about the missing family and it sounded like the perfect story for my magazine." It's so interesting to think that a family disappeared without so much as a clue to where they went or what happened. I was hooked."

"It just seems like such a small story to come all the way from New York to write."

She took another drink from her soda. "This story is really important to me. There's an assistant editor job at my magazine opening up and I'm one of the finalists. Whoever writes the best article for our next issue will get the job. I want it. I think this story could make it for me."

"I think you'll succeed."

"Really? What makes you think that?"

"Well, you seem pretty determined to succeed." He flashed her a smile that melted into her heart.

"Can I ask you a question?" she asked.

"Under the law, I can't stop you.

"Why did you want to be sheriff?"

He took a deep breath before answering. "I grew up around here and then left for college, and then worked for a while in Chicago."

"What did you do in Chicago?" she asked.

"I worked as the head of the Security Department for a big hotel."

"Wow, your first job was as a department head? I'm impressed."

"My degree was in law enforcement and I had connections with the hotel. It didn't work out though. I came back home a couple years ago when I realized the sheriff's office was up for election."

"And, you won."

"I did. I was pleased that the citizens of the county held enough respect and trust in me to elect me sheriff."

She couldn't remember ever being around a man that appeared so humble. Certainly none of the men at her office came close. *Vultures, all of them.*

"I can't find the Murdock file. Are you sure it was in here?" she asked him.

He sat next to her at the table and leaned close to see what she was looking at. There was that scent again: rugged, strong, and sexy. She liked it.

"Let me look." He fumbled through the box. "All right, this is the map, but the rest of the file seems to be missing."

"That's kind of odd. What does the map show?"

"That's the federal geographical area. Legend has it that the Murdock's may have been pushed off of a cliff there and then the murderer started an avalanche of rock to cover their bodies."

"Was the area ever searched?"

"I believe it has been several times over and people still hike there all the time. About a year or so ago, a skeleton was found near the avalanche area."

"Really? Who was it?" she asked.

"An Indian from hundreds of years ago. There should be a newspaper article in there about it." He moved closer and reached for a file at the same time she did. Their hands met.

She felt his breath on her cheek and looked up and found him looking at her. Slowly, their lips touched. The kiss was cold and crisp. She weakened as he put his arm around her and pulled her closer.

"Six-Oh-One, Central Dispatch." His hand-held radio startled them both.

Jaime got up from the chair to retrieve something from her bag and to hide her embarrassment.

"Dispatch, this is Six-Oh-One. Go ahead."

"There's a ten-thirty PI at the eighty-six mile marker on the interstate. Can you assist 619 with traffic control?"

"Roger. ETA will be in about fifteen to twenty minutes." He looked at Jaime. "We have to go."

She had already started putting everything back into her bag. "Just give me a second."

Ben put the lid back on the file box. "I'll come back later and put the box away, but for now I need to get you back to your car so I can get out to that wreck."

"Sure. I'm ready. I think I have everything I need, for now anyway." She tried not to make eye contact with him. She didn't know why she kissed him, or he kissed her, but she liked it. However, she felt very uneasy around him now.

They walked back out to his car and got in. He put it in gear and flipped on the red and blue lights and headed back to the courthouse. Jaime felt excited to be riding in the car with the flashing lights. Quickly, he pulled up next to her car. She got out and before she could say anything, he sped off.

# Chapter Three

Later that evening, Jaime pulled her rental car into the parking lot of the Historical Society's museum. The flyer indicated that the meeting started at seven, but she had taken a nap earlier and overslept causing her to be about thirty minutes late.

She entered the building and could hear voices coming from behind the closed door on the right. *If I can just slip in without interrupting*, she thought. It didn't work. The door creaked when she opened it and all eyes were on her as she stepped into the room.

Sam Morgan, the Society's president stood at the front of the room behind a podium. "Come in Miss Wilson. Please, take a seat." The frustrated tone of his voice confirmed it all: he didn't like her interrupting the meeting. After walking past at least five rows of chairs that sat behind cafeteria-type tables, she took the only available seat located in the front of the nearly full room.

"I'm sorry to interrupt," she whispered as she sat down. She noticed several familiar faces in the crowd. Annie sat in the next seat, Jenny from the restaurant sat on the right side of the room, with Bobby James next to her, and Kenneth Morgan, the newspaper editor sat in the back corner with a pad of paper taking notes. To Jaime's surprise, she spotted Ben standing in the back of the room. She smiled and he nodded.

"As I was saying, everyone's membership dues need to be paid before next month's meeting. Please try and get your money to Sarah as soon as possible. Now, if we have no more business to discuss, we can let our speaker take over the meeting." Sam paused for a few seconds. "Very good. I think most of you know our speaker for the evening. He's our former sheriff and the local expert on the Murdock disappearance, Clayton Spencer.

The crowd applauded as Spencer stepped to the podium. "Thank you." He tried to wave the crowd silent. "Thank you for asking me here. I know everyone is interested in the Murdock family and I hope to help educate you on what happened with the family. I think just about everyone here knows how the story goes." He looked over at Jaime, which embarrassed her. "So, instead of giving a lecture, I'll let you ask me any questions you have."

Jaime took out her small voice recorder so she could tape the questions and answers and put it on the table in front of her.

"Can you tell us about Jacob Katt? Everyone seems to think he had something to do with the Murdock's," someone from the back of the room asked.

"Certainly, it's believed that Katt was in love with the Murdock's daughter, Bonnie. Some even think she might have been pregnant by him and that's what caused the whole thing to blow up between him and the family."

"But, you don't think that happened, do you?" someone else asked.

"No, I don't. If you recall, I spoke with Katt at his home a few months before he took sick. Although I did not ask him directly about their disappearance, he expressed that he never had anything to do with that family, other than telling them to keep their dog tied up. Seems as though their male dog kept coming around when his female dog was in heat."

The crowd laughed. Jaime remained stoic.

"So, who did kill them?" Jaime asked.

The room went silent. "I don't believe I know you, young lady." Spencer directed his comment toward Jaime.

"My name is Jaime Wilson. I'm a writer from *Real Mystery Magazine* and came here to do research for a story about the Murdock family."

"Well, it's nice to meet you. Richard, did you have a question?" Spencer turned his attention to the gentleman on the right side of the room.

"You didn't answer my question," Jaime insisted.

A low mumble went through the room. Spencer looked at Jaime. His eyes pierced through her and she felt his anger. "Like everyone, I have a theory about what happened to the Murdock's," he responded. "But, out of respect for their family, I don't what to say what I believed happened."

Jaime noticed that no one seemed surprised at the former sheriff's answer. She thought best not to pursue it any further.

"Anymore questions?" Spencer asked, looking around the room. No one else spoke. "Well, I thank you for asking me here tonight."

Sam Morgan walked back to the front of the room. "Thank you for coming, Clay. It's always good to have you here. I think that about wraps up the meeting tonight. There's plenty of cookies and coffee in the back of the room. Please help yourself. There's also a bucket in the back for any donations toward the renovation of the building here."

Everyone got up and moved to get some refreshments. Jaime turned off her tape recorder and saw Clayton Spencer quickly walk out the door to leave. Just as quickly, she grabbed her bag and followed him outside.

"Mr. Spencer, may I have a word?" she called.

He ignored her and kept walking.

She ran after him, catching him just as he put his key into the lock of his car.

"Please, Mr. Spencer. I would love to ask you some more questions for my article, if we could set up a time."

Spencer turned around and took a step toward her. "You best mind your own business, sweet thing. You stick your nose in where people don't want it and you could find yourself in a heap of trouble, if you get what I mean."

Jaime knew a threat when she heard it and was about to respond when someone interrupted.

"Is there a problem here?" She recognized Sheriff Ben's deep voice and was relieved to hear it.

Spencer took a step back to his car. "There's no problem, if she will leave me alone." He stared at Ben. "You have a job to do Sheriff, and that is to keep her from harassing me. If you can't do that, then I'll see to it that someone does." He got in his car, slammed the door shut and quickly drove off.

"Harassing him? He threatened me. Twice, he threatened me twice. You heard him," Jaime raved.

"Calm down. He's a harmless old man. I wouldn't worry about him."

"I'm not worried about him, but I don't like threats being thrown my way so viciously."

"Where's your car? I'll walk you to it."

"It's over there." She motioned toward the darkest part of the parking lot where no security lights were.

She felt him touch her back and guide her toward her car, leaving his hand there while they walked.

"The former sheriff doesn't seem to like you very much."

"Nope, he doesn't."

"Why is that?"

"Could be because I beat him in the last election." Just as they neared her car, Ben grabbed her by the arm to stop and pulled a small flashlight out of his pocket. He shined the light on her front tire.

"Flat?" she exclaimed.

"Not just flat, but purposely flat," he bent over the tire and pulled something out of it. "Someone stuck a small screwdriver into your tire."

"Someone doesn't like me asking questions, do they?"

"It sure seems like that way. Let's go over to my car."

He unlocked his patrol car and opened the passenger door for her to get in. Once he sat inside, he called on his radio. "Dispatch, six-oh-one."

"Go ahead, six-oh-one."

"There's a newer model Saturn, blue in color in the county museum parking lot. Someone has flattened at least one tire on it. Have six-nineteen come over here, and call a wrecker to come fix the tire. Make sure and tell them to check the other tires, too."

"Roger, six-oh-one. Six-nineteen is on station and said he would be there in a few minutes. Wrecker One will be notified."

"Roger." Ben turned to Jaime. "How about we have a cup of coffee until your tire is fixed?" he asked.

"That sounds really good. I'm kind of cold right now."

Ben drove them to the truck stop at the interstate. "This is the only place open this time of night."

"Any place is fine, as long as the coffee's hot."

They got out and went inside. Truck drivers occupied a few of the tables and country music blared from the jukebox by the front door. Ben led her to a booth in the back corner of the room. It didn't take long for a waitress to come over to take their order.

"Coffee, please," Jaime requested.

"I'll take the same, and do you have any apple pie tonight?" Ben asked.

"Yes, we do," the waitress replied.

"Would you like some pie?" Ben asked Jaime.

"That sounds really good."

"Two pieces of apple pie please, and could you warm them up, too?"

"Would you like a scoop of ice cream on it?"

"None for me," Ben answered and Jaime agreed.

The waitress thanked them for their order and walked away.

Neither of them spoke a word. Jaime wondered if his thoughts were back at the old courthouse when they shared the kiss. She couldn't get that out of her mind.

"You're going to have to be very careful while you're here," he finally murmured.

"Why, because of the flat tire? Please, I come from New York City. Someone flattening my tire is minor."

"That's exactly why you need to be more careful. You aren't from around here. You don't know who anyone is or who might want to hurt you."

The waitress brought their coffee and pie, setting both in front of them and then walking away.

"Why would someone want to hurt me?"

"There are some people around her that don't like outsiders snooping around. You're looking into the Murdock family disappearance and some things are better left alone." He took a bite of his pie.

Jaime did the same. She watched his strong jaw move as he chewed his pie. His chin, with a slight dimple, came to a point and then square off. She thought about what he said. Could he know something about the family's disappearance that he wasn't telling? Why else would he say that?

"This pie is really good," she commented.

"Yeah, Millie, back in the kitchen, makes them herself. She's a great cook."

"I think I'm going to the newspaper office tomorrow. I met the editor earlier today and he said I could come look through their files for articles about the Murdock's." She took another bite of pie and the waitress came by with the coffee pot to freshen their cups.

"From now on, you need to keep your eyes open for trouble. Before getting into your car, make sure all the tires are okay and that no one is hiding in the backseat. Keep your cell phone with you, too. Here, keep this number handy." He took out a pen and wrote a phone number on the napkin. "This is my cell phone. If you need help, call me right away."

Now, she felt a little scared. "You're really serious about this, aren't you?"

"I don't want anything to happen to you."

She thought back to the kiss earlier in the day. "Today, at the old courthouse, you kissed me. Why?"

He blushed and hesitated before answering. "I-I don't know why. I shouldn't have done it. I'm sorry." He took a drink of his coffee to hide his nervousness

"Don't be," she blurted out. *Oh my gosh. I can't believe I said that.*

"What?"

She didn't know what to say, but she knew by the heat from her skin that she was blushing. "It will be our secret."

Ben looked around the room. "It's getting a little crowded in here to talk. Let's drive back to your car and see if they have a new tire on there yet?"

At ten o'clock, the road had no traffic. He drove slowly back to the museum.

"I didn't want to talk back at the restaurant because everyone wants to hear what the sheriff is saying to the pretty lady."

*He called me a pretty lady.* "I guess all eyes are usually on you."

"And, it makes it even worse because I'm single. I can't begin to tell her how many of the older ladies in town are constantly trying to marry me off." He laughed.

"That sounds like my grandmother. She's always asking me if I'm seeing anyone."

"Are you?"

She couldn't believe what she just heard. "No, I'm not. I don't have much time for romance. My evenings are usually spent researching or writing a story. And, as for dates..." She could barely talk from laughing. "The men I have gone out with aren't usually interested in hearing me talk about the recent gory murder mystery I'm researching. They don't want to know about blood splatters, fingerprints, and DNA. They get enough of that from television."

Suddenly, Ben turned the car in to the parking lot of a school and shut the motor off. "You just haven't met the right guy yet."

"You think?"

"Oh yeah." He scooted a little closer to her. "You need someone that understands all of that kind of stuff. Take blood splatter, for instance. Depending on which way the blood is going could determine where the perpetrator stood." He again moved a little closer. "Now, fingerprints can be tricky." He took her hand and held it up. "If you don't lift it correctly, you won't get a print good enough for matching purposes." One more move and she could feel the heat of his body right next to her. "As for DNA, well there are several ways that it can be left on the body." He leaned down, placed his hand under her chin, and kissed her.

Then, Jaime felt his hand lying on her leg. Slowly, he moved his hand up her body. His familiar scent filled her lungs, intoxicating her, and his lips were rough, a bit chapped tonight, and she tasted coffee. He shifted in the seat and his hand finally found its way to her breast, but she pushed him away at that touch.

"I think we are going a little fast," she suggested.

"I'm sorry. It's just so nice finding someone like you here in town. I didn't mean to take advantage of the situation."

"No, it's just a little soon for me."

"We should probably be getting back to your car. I'm sure they have the tire fixed by now." He moved back over to the driver's side and started the car. When they pulled into the museum parking lot, they found the deputy and the wrecker driver letting her car down off the jack.

They got out of the patrol car and walked over to the two men. "Chris," Ben acknowledged the wrecker driver.

Jaime recognized the wrecker driver as the owner of the garage that she met earlier in the day.

"Evening, Sheriff. I replaced the lady's flat tire and checked the others. The valve stem had been pulled on one other tire, but it looks like whoever did this, didn't have time to mess with the rest of them."

"How much do I owe you for the repair and service call?" Jaime asked.

"I haven't really had time to write up your ticket."

"Why don't you wait until tomorrow? I'm sure Miss Wilson will stop by your garage to pay it"

"Of course, I will. I know right where it is since I was there already today."

She looked at Ben, who had a confused look on his face. "This afternoon, one of your deputies was kind enough to find that my tail light had been broken and suggested that I go to Chris's garage to get it fixed so he wouldn't have to write me a ticket."

"I see," Ben stared suspiciously at Deputy Mark Stokes.

"It wasn't me," Stokes said.

"I'll check into it first thing in the morning. I don't run a department like that."

"Thank you." She then turned to the wrecker driver. "So, my car is ready to go?"

"Yes, ma'am, it is."

She got into her car and started the engine. Ben stood outside the door and she rolled down the window.

He leaned down and stuck his head through. "Want me to follow you back to your cabin to make sure you get there safely?" he asked.

"No, but thanks. I'll be fine." She remembered how eager his hands had been a moment ago.

"Remember, call me if you need anything." He stood back up.

"Thanks." She drove off.

Jaime had walked the streets of New York at night many times and never felt scared, but the drive to the cabin tonight had her worried. She had never seen a night so dark. The lights of the city kept New York brightly lit at night, but out in the country the only lights were from the occasional house she passed during her drive. The quarter moon didn't reflect much light on this night, but at least she could see a lot stars in the clear sky, which was something she rarely saw in the city.

Without warning, her headlights came upon a deer standing in the middle of the road. Slamming on the brakes, she swerved to miss the beautiful animal that fortunately ran off the road and into a grove of trees. Her heart raced at the close call. A few minutes later, she turned into the driveway of the Buckhorn Cabins and followed the narrow lane to her cabin.

Each cabin had a security light next to it, but the one next to her cabin was out tonight. She'd make a mental note to tell the owners tomorrow. Walking carefully, she made her way to the front door. No light on the porch either, she'd forgot to leave it turned on. After unlocking the door, she stepped in and flipped the light on.

The cabin had been ransacked.

# Chapter Four

Jaime looked around the tousled cabin. Cushions from the couch and chair had been thrown everywhere. The lamp and other items from the table were on the floor. Taking no chances, she ran back to her car, got in, and locked the doors.

She immediately started dialing her phone. "Ben, its Jaime. Someone has been in my cabin and wrecked everything." She started the car and turned on the lights to see more of the area around her. "No, I'm in the car right now. Can you come here?" She looked around the car to see if she could spot anyone close. "Okay. I'll meet you at the main office."

She closed her cell phone and drove to the office and waited with Mr. Ferguson until Ben arrived.

\* \* \* \*

Ben walked out of the cabin's bedroom and into the living room where Jaime and Mr. Ferguson stood waiting. "It looks like the sliding glass door in the bedroom was unlocked. I can't find any evidence of a forced entry."

"I never opened that door. I only used the front door," Jaime retorted.

"Ned, can you change the locks on the door tomorrow?" Ben asked.

"Sure can. I want to make sure Miss Wilson is safe," he replied.

"I think she'll be fine here tonight. You go on back and let Helen know everything's okay. I'll have a deputy drive out here a couple times tonight on patrol."

"Thanks, Ben. We'd appreciate it." Ferguson turned and walked out of the cabin, leaving Ben and Jaime alone.

"It's almost midnight. Do you have any idea where you're going to stay tonight?" Ben asked.

She walked into the bedroom and started throwing things in her suitcase. "I'll go the hotel I saw at the Interstate, next to that restaurant we were at earlier." She kept packing.

"You can't go there. It's probably full and if it isn't, you don't have any business out there with the type of people that stay there at night."

She stopped packing and turned to him. "Where do you suggest I go then?"

He let out a deep breath before answering. "You can stay at my place."

Probably for the first time in her life, Jaime became momentarily speechless. "I'm not sure that is such a good idea," she finally said. "I don't really know you very well."

"I'm the sheriff. Who are you going to trust more than me?"

"There's that little matter of kissing me."

"I apologize for that. I was out of line, but you're such a beautiful woman. I promise to keep my lips and my hands to myself. But," he added, "Can you say you didn't like it?"

She couldn't, but didn't want to admit it.

"I have an extra bedroom and it has a lock on the door."

"Is that to keep whoever did this out, or to keep you out?" she joked, looking around the ransacked room.

"Both, I reckon."

She thought about it for a moment.

"There's not a safer place to stay in the county," he added.

"Okay. I guess I'll take you up on your offer, on one condition."

"What's that?"

"I want the key to the bedroom."

"Deal."

By the time she finished packing, the deputy had arrived to take the report for the break-in.

"I haven't found anything missing," she told him. "I had my laptop, tape recorder, and camera with me."

"Mark, photograph this mess in here and then talk with Ned at the office. He may need a copy of your report for the insurance company in case he finds any damage," Ben instructed.

"Yes, sir."

"Oh, and tell him Miss Wilson will be back tomorrow for the rest of her things. She's decided to stay somewhere else tonight."

Jaime and Ben walked out of the cabin. He put her suitcase in the back of her car. "Follow me to my house."

"How far is it?"

"Not far. Maybe twenty minutes."

During the drive to Ben's home, she decided to call Gabrielle. "I'm sorry to call so late, Gabby."

"That's okay. I've not gone to bed yet."

She looked at the clock in the car that showed twelve-fifteen.

"You aren't going to believe what has happened? First, someone vandalized a tire on my car tonight and when I finally got back to the cabin where I'm staying, it had been broken into."

"Oh my gosh, are you okay?"

"I'm fine. Ben thinks that someone doesn't like me snooping around about the Murdock family."

"Ben? As in Sheriff Ben?"

"Yes, he was with me when I found my tire and he came after I discovered the mess at the cabin."

"Sounds like you have a knight in shining armor to protect you," Gabby teased.

"Not really a shining knight. He seems to be more into Earth tones," she laughed.

"Where are you now? It sounds like you are driving."

"I am. I'm following Ben to his house." Following him, she made a right turn onto another road.

"You're going to his house?"

"He didn't think it would be safe for me to stay at the cabin tonight and insisted I go with him to his place," she explained.

This time, Gabrielle laughed. "I thought you were smarter than that, girl. Haven't you learned anything about men? I don't care if he's a cop or not, he only wants one thing."

"Normally, I would agree, but he isn't like that."

"They're all like that, sweetie."

The right turn signal on Ben's car started flashing and she followed him as he turned into a driveway.

"I have to go, Gabby. We just got to his house. Don't worry about me and I'll call you tomorrow."

"Okay. Be careful."

"I will." By the time she hung up from the call, Ben stood next to her car and opened the door.

"Who were you talking to?" he asked.

"A co-worker and my best friend. I call her every night to check in."

"That's good. Come on inside. It looks like it's going to start raining again at any minute." The sound of thunder could be heard rumbling off in the distance.

There were no lights on in or around the house and Jaime thought that strange. Ben carried her suitcase to the porch, opened the door, and immediately turned on an outside light. A large front porch ran along the whole front length of the house, which appeared to be a ranch style.

"Sorry about the mess," he apologized, once inside.

There was no doubt that a man lived alone in this house. She really wouldn't call it messy, just comfortable. Obviously, he didn't entertain often. Several newspapers were on top of the coffee table and it looked as though that morning's breakfast dishes were still sitting on top of the papers.

A couple pairs of socks and shoes sat next to the couch and she noticed a bucket of ashes next to the fireplace that had never been removed.

"Your house looks fine."

Suddenly, a small dog came running into the room barking and growling at Jaime. She jumped behind Ben to keep him between her and the dog.

"Jake, down." The dog immediately went to a sitting position and stopped barking. "Sorry, this is Jake. Don't worry about him, he's more bark than bite."

Jaime stepped around Ben and bent over to pet the dog. Eventually, he rolled over begging for his stomach to be rubbed. "Cute dog."

"He's a Jack Russell terrier. I adopted him from the local animal shelter. They found him wandering along side of a road with an injured leg, probably hit by a car." He opened a door at the back of the living room and went in. "Your room is right here."

She walked over to the door and waited while he put her bag on the bed and came back out.

"Still not sure you trust me?" he asked.

"Just being careful, I guess."

He walked over to the desk at the side of the room and opened a drawer. From inside, he brought a key and handed it to Jaime. "This is the only key to the bedroom door."

She felt a little ashamed as she took the key. "Thanks."

"The bathroom is down that way on the right." He pointed to a dark hallway. "You'll find clean towels in a closet inside and if you walk all the way down the hallway, it leads to the kitchen and a dining room. If you're hungry, I think I have some turkey lunchmeat in the refrigerator."

"I'm not hungry, but I'm really tired. If you don't mind, I think I'll clean up a bit and then go to bed."

"Of course, it's late. I'm sorry. I keep odd hours and don't think about other people's routine."

She walked down the hall to the bathroom and closed the door behind her. When she came out, she found Ben sitting on the couch with his sock feet propped up on the coffee table next to an opened can of beer, while he read the local newspaper. Jake slept on the floor next to him. He stood up when he heard her walk into the room.

"Thank you for letting me stay here. I hope I won't be too much trouble."

"You won't be any trouble at all. Here, you will probably need this." He handed her another key. "It's a key to the house so you can come and go as you please."

"Thanks. I should get to bed now."

"Good-night."

"Good-night." She closed the door and started to turn the lock on the doorknob, but stopped. She decided to leave it unlocked. She did trust him, or was the real reason that she hoped he would come in during the night?

She pulled the covers down and crawled into bed. The cool, clean, crisp sheets were a welcome comfort and in no time, she had fallen fast asleep.

The alarm Jaime had set on her cell phone sounded at six o'clock the next morning. Now, she wished she hadn't scheduled that hike with Bobby James to the Murdock homestead this morning. She forced herself to get out of bed and dress. When she opened the door to the living room, the aroma of freshly made coffee hit her. With that, she perked up a little and made her way to the kitchen. "Good morning, Jake," she said to the dog, who was lying on a mat by the back door.

Next to the coffee pot she found a large mug and a note.

*I left breakfast for you in the microwave. Enjoy, Ben.*

Jaime smiled when she opened the microwave to find a plate with scrambled eggs, three pieces of bacon, two slices of toast, and some hash browns. She closed the door and started the microwave to heat for a few seconds while she made a quick trip to the bathroom. Once back, she poured herself some coffee and then shut off the coffee pot. She took the food and coffee into the living room and sat on the couch. "If Ben eats in here, so can I."

She turned the television on and watched a little of the news while she ate. The weatherman predicted a cool October day. All the rain had passed and the sun would come out later in the morning.

Quickly, she finished breakfast and left for her morning meeting. She had no trouble finding her way back to the highway and on to the Corner Café restaurant where she found Jenny pouring coffee into a large travel mug for Bobby at the table by the door.

"Hi, hope I'm not too late."

"Nope, right on time." Bobby was dressed the same as he had been the day before. Apparently, flannel shirt and jeans were the norm for Royal men. When she looked around the busy restaurant, she saw many of them were dressed the same way.

"Would you like some coffee to take with you?" Jenny asked.

She started to say yes, but remembered that they would be walking out in the woods and not the most convenient place to be with a stranger if you had to go to the bathroom. "No, thanks. Maybe when we get back."

"We better get going." Bobby stood up.

Outside, he opened the door of his truck for her to get in. She buckled her seatbelt as Bobby started the truck. "Before we head out, remember we'll be on private property and could get in a heap of trouble if we get caught," he warned.

"I know. Let's go."

They pulled out of the restaurant parking lot and started east on the highway. About a mile down the road, she saw an approaching police car. She quickly put her sunglasses and a hat on. Sure enough, she saw Ben driving the car and hoped he hadn't seen her. Of all things to do, Bobby waved at him.

"Wearing that hat is probably a good idea. It's still wet in the woods and that'll keep the drops from falling on your head."

*Not exactly why I'm wearing it, but that will do.* "How far will we have to walk to get to the homestead?"

"A couple miles. It's pretty flat, so it should be an easy walk."

"Good." The drive into the country gave her time to think. Someone in this town did not want her writing about the Murdock family. After her vandalized tire and nearly turning the inside of the cabin upside down, she wondered what length they would go to in order to keep her from writing her story. Was writing this story important enough to continue her research?

Gabrielle had told her that Jonathan had been spending a lot of time in the editor's office. Kissing butt, no doubt. She laughed to herself at that image, but wouldn't put something like that past him to get what he wanted.

"Something funny?" Bobby asked.

"Just thinking about some co-workers at the magazine. How much farther?" she asked.

Bobby pulled the truck off onto the side of the road. "We're here."

She looked around at the isolated area and suddenly got a bad feeling. No houses were in sight, only a field on the right and woods on the left. "Where are we?"

"Well, it's kind of hard to explain to someone not from around here. We'll be walking down that little road there and into those woods." He pointed to a line of trees at the far end of the field. "Once in those trees, we'll walk down a trail and then cross another small field to another set of trees. The house we're looking for is in that last set of trees."

They got out of the truck and started walking down what appeared to be a little used dirt road. "What else is there besides the house?" she asked.

"The barn's still there."

They reached the first set of trees and the trail started heading downward.

"Watch your step, its kind of slick with all the mud left from last night's rain," Bobby warned.

"Do you know anything about Clayton Spencer investigating the Murdock's disappearance?"

"Yeah. He received a weird letter in the mail once that wasn't signed and it gave some clues about the Murdock disappearance."

"Did he check up on the clues?" she asked.

"He told people he did."

They finally reached the second field and started walking across it to the last row of trees. Bobby walked so fast she had been taking two steps to his one.

"Can we stop for a minute?" she asked.

"Sure. We can sit on that big rock over there." They walked to the large, flat rock to rest a bit.

"Bobby, is there anyone around here that would want to keep what really happened to the Murdock's a secret?" she asked.

"I wouldn't know who. But, the Cook family sure doesn't like anyone snooping around the property. That's why we are coming in the back way. It'd be a lot easier if we just drove to their house."

"Are they hiding something out there?"

"Huh? Oh, no, I don't think so."

Jaime made a mental note to see what she could find out about the Cook family. "I think I've rested enough, let's get going."

It didn't take long for them to reach the second row of trees and start down another trail.

"From here on, you need to be quiet. We are close to the Cook's home and we don't want them to know we're here," Bobby whispered.

They walked down the trail for a few more yards and then she saw an old, run down house. "Is that it?" she whispered.

"Yeah. We can walk around the front if you want a picture."

"I definitely want a picture."

Reaching the front of the house seemed like a walk through time. A swing on one side of the porch swayed in the breeze while a wooden rocking chair sat still on the other side. The chopping block had an axe buried in the top of it with split wood on the ground around it.

"Has someone been living here?" she asked Bobby.

"I've hiked out here since I was a kid and it's always been this way. Nothing ever changes."

She snapped a few pictures with her camera flash going off with each shot she took. "I want to look inside through the windows."

"Okay, but be quick. I don't like being out here in the open so long. With the leaves off of the trees, the Cook's might see that flash of yours going off."

Jaime carefully walked up to the old house that stood near a newer home with a barn between the two. She took a few pictures through the windows. The inside of the house looked like no one had been there in years. Perhaps left just the way it was when the Murdock's had last been there. She stood at the front door and couldn't resist trying the knob. The door opened.

"I don't think that's a good idea," he warned.

"I'll just take one picture of the inside and then we'll go." She took one step into the house.

"I don't think that's a good idea," he related again.

"You should listen to the boy," a deep voice echoed from behind them.

She knew that voice.

"Come on out."

Jaime turned to see Ben standing at the corner of the old house, handcuffing Bobby behind his back. "What are you doing?" she asked, walking over to them.

"Arresting him for trespassing. You're next."

"What!"

"Didn't you see the No Trespassing sign?" Ben asked.

"Yes, but..."

"Then you should have turned back. Now, turn around."

Jaime put her camera on the porch and turned around for Ben to handcuff her. "This isn't exactly what I in mind when I thought of you handcuffing me," she mumbled to him.

He didn't answer, but instead picked up her camera and led them through the trees to his police car that was parked in front of the other house. She assumed it belonged to the Cook family. A woman in a housedress stood on the front porch.

"They won't be back out here again, Mrs. Cook," Ben called to the lady.

"Thanks, Sheriff."

He opened the back door of his car and Bobby got in. Before Jaime got in, she looked up at Ben. "I'm sorry."

He didn't answer, but put his hand on top of her head so she wouldn't bump it as he guided her into the car.

"Where's your truck, Bobby?" Ben asked.

"Over on Jackson Road."

"I'm sorry about this, Bobby," Jaime said.

"Don't worry about it. It's not like I haven't seen the inside of that jail before."

Ben picked the microphone to his radio. "Dispatch, Six-Oh-One."

"Go ahead Six-Oh-One."

"Call Wrecker One and have him tow in a red Chevy pickup that's parked on Jackson Road."

"Roger," the dispatcher answered.

No one spoke during the rest of the ride to the Sheriff's Department.

Once inside the sally port, Jaime and Bobby were separated. The female deputy took Jaime to the female side of the jail for booking. Her handcuffs were removed and she emptied her pockets of the small wallet, cell phone, and car keys and then the deputy search her.

After being fingerprinted, the deputy gave her some clothes. "You need to put these on and hand your shirt and jeans out to me. I'll put them in a bag for you to change back in to when you bond out."

Jaime had to undress in front of the deputy, putting her clothes into a large clear plastic bag she held open. "When do I get to call someone?" she asked.

"As soon as you get dressed, I'm to take you to the Sheriff. You can call someone at that time."

Jaime put on the bright orange jumpsuit with the word "prisoner" printed on the back, and followed the deputy to the sheriff's office. She knocked on the door. "Come in."

The deputy opened the door. "I have Miss Wilson here, sir."

"Have her come in. I'll see that she gets to a cell when I'm finished speaking with her. Thank you."

The deputy opened the door wider for Jaime to enter the office. Ben got up. "Sit down," he motioned to a chair in front of his desk and walked around and closed the door. "What were you doing out there?" He sat back down behind his desk.

"I needed pictures for my story."

"Why didn't you ask permission first?"

"I was told the family that owned the property didn't want anyone out there?"

"Who told you that? Bobby James? And, how the hell did you get mixed up with him anyway? For all you know, he could have been the person that vandalized your tire or wrecked the cabin!"

"None of that is any of your business. When do I get to call someone to bail me out?"

"Right now." He picked up his phone and slammed it down on the desk in front of her.

She jumped when the phone hit the desk. "Could I have some privacy please?" she asked.

"No. You're a prisoner and I can't leave you alone in here. Push nine and then dial your number."

Jaime did as told and after several rings someone finally answered. "I need to speak to Gabrielle Santoro, please. Tell her its Jaime Wilson."

Gabby came on the line almost immediately.

"Gabby, I need some help. I've been arrested."

"What?" Gabby answered. "What happened?"

"It's a long story I can't go into now, but could you please bail me out?"

"Of course, what do I do?"

She looked at Ben. "How do I go about getting bailed out of here?"

"She can speak with the clerk outside and she can take care of it."

"I'm going to put you through to the clerk here at the jail and they will tell you what to do. Oh, and Gabby, do not let Jonathon know about this."

"Don't worry. I'll have you out of there in no time," Gabby promised.

Jaime held the receiver for Ben to take. He put the phone on hold and then buzzed the clerk over the intercom to take the call.

"I'll have someone take you to a cell until the paperwork is finished to bond you out."

"I'll need to find somewhere else to stay after I'm out of here."

"Why?"

"Why? I'm sure you don't want a criminal staying with you." She got up.

He did the same and walked to the door. "You're still in danger and my house is where you need to be." He opened the door and called for a jailer to take Jaime to a holding cell.

# Chapter Five

The bond money came in later that afternoon, enabling Jaime to be released. When Ben arrived at home that evening, he saw her car in the driveway. Once inside the house, the smell of dinner floated in the air. He found her in the kitchen standing at the stove. Both her shirt and jeans were tight enough to show the perfect curve of her body. She had pulled her long brunette hair into a ponytail, exposing her sensuous neck, a part of the body he had trouble resisting.

"What smells good?" he asked.

"Just something I threw together from what I could find in the house. Do you like Beef Fried Rice?"

"Yes, but it's been a while since I've had it." He noticed the table was set, complete with wine glasses.

"Well, you're in for a treat then. Why don't you go get cleaned up for dinner? Everything should be ready when you get back."

He picked up her glass of wine sitting on the counter next to her and sniffed it. "I don't recall having any wine in the house."

"I stopped and bought some on the way here."

"I don't drink wine." He sat the glass down, turned and left the room.

In the master bathroom, he took off his uniform and washed up in the sink. The water cooled his face and helped clear his mind, at least for a second. He dried off, his rough five o'clock shadow catching on the towel. He dressed in his usual off-duty clothes, a t-shirt and jeans and then sat on the bed to put on his slippers.

Once back in the kitchen, he opened the refrigerator to get out a bottle of beer.

"Sit down, it's ready." She took the platter full of rice to the table.

Both of them sat down and she spooned the rice onto both of their plates.

"I baked a pie for dessert."

"You cook, you bake, what else do you do?" he asked, taking a bite of food.

"I'm a writer."

"You're a writer who takes too many risks," he replied.

"That's your opinion," she shot back.

"You need to be more careful around here."

"Why? What is so important about the Murdock disappearance that the people around here don't want me digging into?" She took a drink of her wine.

"Folks around here don't want outsiders coming and snooping around after your story is published. Kind of like you did at the Cook place today." He took another bite of food and swallowed. "If you had told me you wanted to see the place, I would have talked to them and probably been able to take you out there to look around."

"Can you do that?" she asked.

"Not now. You go about things all wrong."

She didn't respond. Both ate their dinner in silence for a few moments.

"Who's Jonathan?" he asked.

"What?"

"When you were talking to your friend on the phone today you said not to tell Jonathan."

"He's the person I'm competing against for the Assistant Editor job," she answered.

"Why wouldn't you want him knowing you were arrested? There must be more to it."

"He's my competitor at work."

Ben tilted his head in doubt.

"Okay, he and I went out a few times when I first started working at the magazine. But, I learned real fast that he's a jerk and now we're only co-workers." She got up and took her plate to the kitchen sink.

Ben did the same, but put his plate in the sink by putting his arms around her from behind. She turned quickly and he found himself face-to-face with her. He wrapped his arms around her and began kissing her. Their kiss deepened and his arms held her tighter.

Then, the phone rang and the kiss ended. "I have to get that."

"You have to?"

"It could be work." He walked over to the phone by the doorway, leaving her at the sink. "Hunter."

Looking at his watch, he listened to the person on the other end of the line. "Okay. I'll be there in about fifteen minutes." He hung up the phone.

"You have to leave?" she asked.

"Yes. Keep the door locked and don't open it for anyone except me, and keep Jake inside with you."

"Are you trying to scare me?"

"I'm just taking precautions. I shouldn't be long. Do you still have my cell phone number?"

"Yes."

"Good. Call me if there's any problem."

She followed him to the living room, where he got a gun out of the desk drawer and slipped it on his belt behind his back. He put on a jacket to cover it and walked to the door to leave. Ben smiled back at her. "Lock this behind me."

The phone call he received had been from Sam Morgan, the County Historian, asking him to come to his house for a meeting about Jaime. When Ben arrived at Sam's house, he found the meeting had already started. In addition to Sam, Mark Stokes, his brother Chris, Jake Ferguson, Clayton Spencer, and a few other men sat around the room.

"Hello, Ben. Please, come in and join us," Morgan greeted.

He said hello to everyone and sat down in the chair on the side of the living room.

"She just needs to leave," Spencer whaled. "And, she needs to do that right now. We don't need anyone snooping around our town."

"I agree," another man confirmed. "When my mother called me and told me that woman had been looking around my place without permission, I got madder then hell. She's got no respect for other people's property."

"Malcolm, did she do any damage out there?" Ben asked Mr. Cook.

"Well, no, no damage, but she could have. If you hadn't got out there when you did, there's no telling what she would have done."

Ben got up and walked over to pour himself a cup of coffee from the pot that sat on the table next to the kitchen door. "You didn't press charges on Bobby James, but you did on Miss Wilson. Why?"

"Bobby wasn't going to hurt anything. She probably bribed him to take her out there. She's not from around here, so why shouldn't I keep those charges on her?"

"Because, you stupid fool, once she gets an attorney to show the judge that you were prejudice against her, the judge will dismiss the charges."

Clayton Spencer stood up. "Ben, you act like you are taking her side of this."

"No, sir. I'm just trying to be fair and equal, so everyone can see the whole picture."

"You sure about that?" Sam Morgan asked, squinting his eyes. "You sure you aren't the one showing prejudice? Isn't that pretty little thing staying at your place now?"

Ben didn't think anyone knew that Jaime was staying with him. Then, it hit him that his deputy had to list where she was now staying on his report about the break-in. He looked over at Mark, who immediately looked down at the floor.

"She is staying at my place, as a guest, nothing more," he answered. "Someone vandalized her car during the historical society meeting and then when she got back to her cabin at the Ferguson's, it had been ransacked. She needed somewhere safe to stay and I suggested my place."

"I didn't know you were in the habit of taking in strays, Sheriff," Morgan sneered.

Ben didn't answer, but instead had a question for all of them. "Do any of you know who would want her out of town so badly that they would vandalize her car and cabin?"

"Are you accusing one of us of doing that?" Morgan asked.

"I'm just asking the question."

No one answered.

"Just so you all know, Miss Wilson will be staying at my place until she has completed all of her research into the Murdock family disappearance." He sat his coffee down and started toward the door, but stopped before exiting. "And, if anything happens to her, or if anyone tries to hurt her, you all will be the first people I come and question." With that, he walked out the door slamming it behind him.

Normally, Ben could control his temper, but this time he let it get the best of him. "Damn it." He hit the steering wheel of his car as he drove down the road. To clear his head before going home, he took a side trip down to the parking area that overlooked the river. *She got to me and I let it happen.* He tried to convince himself that he was doing the right thing. *She's beautiful and I like being around her. She's just the type of woman I could spend the rest of my life with. But, she has her own career and a long-distance relationship would never work.* For her safety, he decided he would help her get her story finished, so she could leave before anything else happened to her. Having made his decision, he started his car and drove home.

Back at his house, he stepped up on the porch and found an envelope stuck on the screen door. Opening it, he read the note inside. "Jaime!" He quickly unlocked the door and found her sitting on the couch petting Jake.

"What's wrong?" she asked.

"Was someone here?"

"I thought I heard someone on the porch, but I stayed in the kitchen until I heard a car drive off. I think Jake's barking scared them away."

He sat down on the couch next to her and showed Jaime the note.

*You made a mistake bringing that writer woman into your home. Don't make it your last mistake. Send her back to the city or else.*

She read it then looked up at him. "Someone is threatening you because of me?"

"They're threatening both of us. I want you to leave. This story isn't important enough for you to risk your life."

"Hell no. I'm not about to leave, especially now. Someone in this town knows something about the Murdock disappearance and I'm not leaving until I find out who and what it is," she promised.

"A lot of people in this town want you out. I just left a meeting where several of the men in this town ordered me to tell you to leave."

"And, you just did what they asked, didn't you?" She got up off the couch.

"No, that's not what I meant." He jumped up and grabbed her by the shoulders. "I don't want anything to happen to you."

"You have a funny way of saying that." She walked away from him.

"I like you, I like you a lot," he confessed. "I would like nothing better than for you to care about me in the same way. But, I'm willing to give up that chance and see you leave than risk some stupid bastard hurting you when all they are trying to do is scare you off."

"Too much happened this week for me to think clearly. I'm going to go to bed. I have to get up early and go to the newspaper office to look through their archives." She turned toward the bedroom, but stopped. "Was the newspaper editor one of the men at the meeting tonight?"

"No."

"Well, that's good. Good-night." She disappeared into her bedroom and closed the door.

Ben sat back down on the couch. His dog rested his head on Ben's lap. "Jake, what am I going to do? I don't want this to end up like Chicago."

Early the next morning, Ben woke up from his sleep. He cleared his head and realized he had fallen asleep on the couch. A blanket had mysteriously appeared over him during the night. Jaime must have come out during the night and covered him with it. He looked over toward her room and saw the door was open.

He quickly got up and looked in her room. Empty. He went to the kitchen where the smell of coffee got stronger as he got closer. "Jaime." The kitchen was empty, also.

Next to the coffee maker he saw a note. *I left early to have breakfast in town and didn't want to wake you. I'll see you tonight. I promise to stay out of trouble. Jaime.*

* * * *

In town, Jaime walked into the newspaper office. A black-haired lady wearing wire-rimmed glasses sat at the front desk looking through a stack of typed pages. She looked up when Jaime neared her desk. "Can I help you?"

"My name is Jaime Wilson. I'm from *Real Mystery Magazine* and I have an appointment with Kenneth Morgan."

"Please have a seat and I'll tell Mr. Morgan you're here."

Jaime sat down on the vinyl-covered couch on the far side of the room while the secretary made a call.

A few minutes later, the door opened and Kenneth Morgan stepped out. "Miss Wilson, I'm so glad you came. Please come this way and I'll take you to our archive room. It's in the basement."

"Thank you." She stood and followed him through the door and down a long hallway. A familiar smell wavered through air. "I don't think I've smelled paper and ink like that since college."

"I wish I could say that we have caught up with the rest of the publishing world, but even though we have computers, most of our printing is still done the old fashion way."

He stopped at a door at the end of the hallway and unlocked it with a key from his pocket. "Here we are." He opened the door and led her down the steps into the dark basement. At the bottom, he turned on the lights. Rows of file cabinets stood along one wall, each drawer with a red label on the front. Two cabinets, labeled as microfilm, stretched along one wall with readers sitting on tables in the middle of the room.

"I need to see the issues from ten years ago."

"If you look under Murdock in our catalog, you should find the file cabinet number and boxed number of the microfilm film you need. Do you know how to use the reader?" he asked.

"Yes, not everything these days are stored on computer disks. We still have readers in New York." She laughed.

"Well then, I will leave you to your research." He walked back up the steps and she heard the door slam closed.

The sound of the slamming door had an eerie feeling about it, reminding her of that jail cell closing.

Jaime set up her laptop to take notes on and using the reader, in no time, she had found the articles she was looking for.

The first article captured her interest right away.

> *The area around the small village of Darnsly was overrun with police from all over the county after the disappearance of the Murdock family was reported. Sheriff Clayton Spencer led the officers in their search for the missing family as they probed the maze of sandstone caves, sinkholes, and cliffs surrounding the family's home.*
>
> *Maude Lane, mother of Judith Murdock, had reported the family missing after not seeing them for three weeks. After looking around the Murdock's home, Sheriff Spencer found a recently covered excavation in the back yard. After obtaining a shovel, he began digging and discovered the body of the Murdock's dog buried in the shallow grave. The animal had been shot in the head and probably dead for about a week to ten days. There are no suspects at this time.*

"Unbelievable."

"What's unbelievable?" a voice asked from behind her.

She jumped, and turned around quickly. . "Ben, what are you doing here?"

"I'm making sure you're okay." He pulled a chair over next to her and sat down. "Find anything interesting?" He placed his arm on the back of her chair.

"This first article says that Clayton Spencer led the investigation. Do you know what kind of police officer he was?"

Before answering, Ben looked behind him toward the stairs. "From what I have learned from reading his old case files, he wasn't much of a police officer. Most people thought of him as more of a politician than a sheriff."

"I can believe that after reading this first article." She continued reading more articles and typing in notes onto her laptop. Ben sat with her and affectionately rubbed her shoulders or back to help her from being stiff after sitting and typing for a couple hours.

"I think I've read enough for today." She rubbed her eyes.

"Don't do that." He pulled her hands away from her eyes.

"Why?"

"It will make your eyes hurt worse. Let's go back to the house and I will help you relax on the couch and sooth your tired eyes with a cool cloth."

Jaime closed her eyes and imagined herself on the couch with Ben. His hands massaged her neck and shoulders, and later bringing her cool cucumber slices to place on her eyes.

"What are you smiling about?" he asked.

She opened her eyes. "Oh, just daydreaming." She checked her watch. "It's only a little after two. Isn't that a little early for you to be going home?"

"I'm the sheriff and I can go home whenever I want."

"Maybe so, but I feel like all eyes are on us and I don't want the residents of Royal to think I am taking their sheriff away from his duties. Besides, I need to start writing my story. How about we make a date for tonight and I'll let you do whatever you need to do in order to get rid of all my stress." She batted her eyelashes in a flirtatious manner.

"It's a date." He got up from his chair and Jaime started packing her computer away. "So, are you going back to the house to work on your article?"

"No. I was thinking about going to the library to do it."

"Good idea. It would be safer for you there than working alone at the house."

"That's not exactly why I'm going there, but if it makes you happy, that's where I'll be for the next couple hours."

"It makes me happy." He planted a kiss smack in the middle of her forehead.

Once she got everything put away, they headed back up the steps to the main floor of the newspaper office. "I want to find Mr. Morgan and thank him for the use of his archive."

"His office is back this way." Ben led her to the rear of the building.

Jaime knocked at the open doorway when they reached his office. "Mr. Morgan?"

"Miss Wilson, please come in."

She walked in with Ben behind her.

"Well, well, I guess the rumors are true," Morgan scoffed.

"Rumors?" she inquired.

"Why you two are the talk of the town. The new romance that's brewing. Didn't you know? All eyes are upon you two."

"Great." Ben shook his head.

"I take it you didn't want people knowing. You know how the gossips love a good story to tell, Ben."

"There's no romance, Sam. Miss Wilson needed a place to stay after her cabin was vandalized and I offered her a room at my place. That's all, and I'd appreciate it if you would let the gossips know that, too."

"I'll do just that the next time I hear that rumor."

Jaime stiffened, but smiled at Sam. "I wanted to thank you for letting me use your archive, Mr. Morgan. I found a treasure of information in your files, and I will make sure and note that in my article."

"You're very welcome and if you need anything else, please feel free to come back."

"I will. Thank you."

She turned and left Morgan's office and headed toward the front of the building to leave, ignoring Ben. She pushed her way out through the front door and out onto the busy street.

"Hey, wait up," Ben called.

Jaime immediately stopped and waited for him in front of the town market.

"What's the rush?"

"Are you sure you want to talk to me out here in public?" she asked. "People will see us."

"What are you talking about?"

"The town gossips. Heaven forbid they see us walking together." She waved her arms about.

Ben grabbed her hand and pulled her into the alley. "Look, this town is full of gossips. Kenneth Morgan's wife is one of the biggest. There's not much more for people to do around her. I said that to Morgan to keep from fueling the fire."

She started to walk away, but he pulled her back.

"I was already questioned at that meeting the other night about you living at my place. I told them you were staying there at my invitation and would remain there until you finished your article. Does that sound like I am afraid to be seen with you?"

She looked down toward the ground."I'm sorry."

Ben reached under her chin and lifted it up so she could look into his eyes. "Now, I believe we have a date for a massage tonight, if you're still interested?"

"Absolutely. I'll run into the market to get something for dinner. What time will you be there?" she asked.

"I'll be home around five." He then kissed her quickly on the lips and they turned to walk out of the alley. They looked across the street and saw Ben's deputy, Mark Stokes, watching them from his car before driving off.

"Will that be a problem for you?" she asked.

"Not if I can help it. See you tonight." Ben walked out of the alley and down the street where he had parked his police car.

* * * *

Jaime went into the market and picked up one of the small plastic baskets to put her items in. She had an uneasy feeling as she walked through the store, like all eyes were watching her. She loaded up on fruit and fresh vegetables, especially cucumbers, and then picked up some ingredients to make dip. At the checkout, a gathering of ladies stood whispering until she approached.

The cashier scanned each item and placed them into a paper grocery sack. "That will be fifteen-dollars and thirty-six cents."

Jaime handed her a twenty-dollar bill and while waiting for her change, she spoke to the others. "You have a beautiful little town here, ladies."

"It's probably a little too slow-paced for you though," one of them suggested.

"You'd have to find a real job around here. There's no writing jobs around our little town," another lady added.

"I'm sure I could do all of my writing here and just email it in to my magazine." She hated snoopy ladies and these comments should really get the gossip lines going. Before leaving the store, she reached down and picked up one of those free real estate magazines with all the local listings in front of all the town gossips. As she left the store, one of the ladies snorted, "I doubt the big city girl could last a month living here in the country."

# Chapter Six

That evening, carrying a grocery sack, Ben walked into his home hoping to find Jaime on the couch. It would have been the perfect way to end a very tiring day, he didn't find her in the living room, nor hear her in the kitchen. Her car was in the driveway, so he knew she must be home. "Jaime!"

No answer. He opened the door to her bedroom and found the bed neatly made, but no Jaime. He began to worry. Down the hallway to the kitchen, he found the back door ajar. Setting the grocery sack on the counter and sliding his hand over the holster of his gun, he stepped outside to see Jaime sitting under a tree playing with Jake.

"Hi." She gave him a wave and walked over to him with Jake following. "How was the rest of your day?"

"It was one of those days where you wished you had another job."

They walked back into the house. "I'm sorry to hear that. Maybe you're the one that needs the massage." She walked over to the kitchen sink and washed her hands.

"Maybe we can take care of both of our needs." He put his arms around her from behind and began kissing her neck.

"Why Sheriff Ben, are you trying to seduce me?" she teased.

He stopped and took a step back. "Not me." They both laughed.

"Well, just in case you were, I made something light for dinner tonight."

"You're spoiling me."

I just put together some fresh veggies with Ranch dip." She took the tray out of the refrigerator and set it on the table.

"That's all?" He saw the disappointed look on her face. "I mean, is there anything else to go with it? Like maybe a sandwich or soup?"

"I only fixed the vegetables. I'm sorry. I should have realized you would want something a little more substantial in order to keep up your stamina." She sat down at the table.

"It's fine and will go perfect with what I brought home." He picked the sack up from the table and pulled out a bottle of wine.

"I didn't think you drank wine."

"I occasionally drink wine...when I'm in certain moods."

"Do you have any cheese?"

"I think there's some in the refrigerator drawer." He walked over to the refrigerator and started searching. "Here it is. That's good thinking. Cheese and crackers will go perfect with the veggies and wine."

He brought the cheese to the table.

"It's still not enough for you, is it?"

"Would you mind if I fried up a couple steaks for us?"

"I'm so sorry. Go right ahead a fix a steak, but only for you. The veggies will be plenty for me."

"You sure you don't mind?" He pulled two fresh red marbled pieces of meat from the grocery sack, placing one in the freezer and the other next to the stove.

"Not at all. Should I put a potato in the microwave for you?"

"No. The steak and vegetables will be enough." He turned the knob on the stove to heat up the grill.

It took no time to hear the sizzle sound when the fresh meat hit the grill.

Jaime munched on carrots and celery while Ben finished grilling the steak and joined her at the table. She poured a glass of wine for him and refilled her glass.

"I've been going over some of my notes from the newspaper office and was wondering if you think I might be able to go back out to the Murdock's old home place again?"

Ben couldn't help but laugh. "You do realize that you still have charges pending on you for trespassing out there?"

"I know, but I thought that maybe if the local sheriff escorted me that the owners might make an exception. I really need to look around out there and maybe take some photos for my article. Could you ask them? Please."

"I don't know how much good it would do. I told you about the meeting last night. Malcolm Cook was there and wasn't too happy about you being on his property." Ben took the last bite of steak.

"Something just doesn't add up. I can't believe the police back then didn't follow up on some leads. Just reading those newspaper articles, I found several leads that should've been checked out."

Ben got up and took his plate to the sink. "You forget, we're not the NYPD. This is a small community with a small department, and that was thirty years ago. The resources we have today were not available back then."

"That's another thing. Why wouldn't Clayton Spencer answer my questions at the Historical Society meeting? He's hiding something. I bet he was in on it."

Ben walked back over to her and leaned down near her face. "You have an unbelievable imagination." He kissed her on the lips then picked up his glass of wine and walked to the living room.

Jaime quickly followed. "It's not my imagination. I'm an investigative reporter and I'm sure Clayton Spencer knows more than he is letting on."

"Let me have your feet," he held his hand out.

Jaime smiled and pivoted around to rest her feet on Ben's lap. He removed her shoes and gently massaged one foot.

"You're tense."

"I've been standing in the kitchen for a long time this afternoon." She moaned slightly. "Oh, that feels really good."

"Scoot down closer and I'll rub your legs, too."

She moved down on the couch a little more until she was almost lying completely down. He switched back and forth between each foot and could feel her muscles relax as he continued.

Ben glanced up at her and even through her thin blouse and bra, he could see her nipples hardening. As his excitement grew, he felt himself grow hard.

Suddenly, he stood up. "Where are you going?" she asked.

He held his hand out to her. She took his hand and he pulled up into an embrace. He kissed her, hard and long. Her lips had the slightest taste of the wine she had sipped earlier.

His tongue slid between her parted lips and she welcomed it. Ben felt himself grow tight inside his jeans. In one quick motion, he swept her up into his arms and carried her to his bedroom. Gently, he placed her on the bed.

Ben lay down next to her, not taking his eyes off of her he began kissing her. Slowly, he moved his hand to her shirt, unbuttoning each with skill and precision.

After finishing the last button, his hand unhooked her bra in the front exposing her pink-tipped breasts. His kisses moved down to her neck as he cupped one breast and tickled the nub with his thumb.

Jaime had managed to unbutton Ben's shirt as well and was working on his zipper, when he helped her along by quickly removing his jeans.

Just as fast, he returned to her by trailing his kisses to her breast. Taking the hardened nipple into his mouth, he began suckling, first one and then the other.

Moving his hand downward, he slowly unzipped her jeans and

slipped his hand inside finding the slick wetness of her excitement. He removed his hand and striped her jeans and panties off in one motion. "You won't need these."

He slowly caressed the downy mound and teased her by titillating her inner thighs.

"Ben, I can't take much more of this. I want you."

"Not quite yet," he whispered into her ear. His hand returned to part her satin flesh and allow one finger to enter her warm wetness. She flinched.

"Oh, Ben."

"Shhhh. Lay still."

"I don't think I can," she answered breathlessly.

He also found it difficult to control himself. His hardness ached, wanting to take her right then.

Her legs moved farther apart; he found her arousal spot. With a swift motion of his finger, he felt her move with him until he couldn't stand it any longer and moved on top.

He slid inside of her and she enveloped him. Soon, they moved together simultaneously until he exploded inside of her.

Their breathing finally slowed to short breaths. Their bodies still intertwined with each other, he kissed her on the cheek.

"Wow, you country boys sure know how to show a girl a good time."

He rolled off of her, but held her closely next to him, caressing her skin. "You are beautiful," he brought her hand to his lips for a kiss. Even in the dim light of the moon coming through the window, he could see that she blushed.

"Let's just go to sleep lying like this," she suggested.

He reached down and pulled the covers of the bed up over them, and soon they both fell asleep together.

* * * *

The next morning, Ben awoke first and looked at her sleeping peacefully. He brushed a few strands of hair from her face and she slowly began to wake up.

"Good morning," he said as she opened her eyes.

"Good morning. What time is it?"

He looked over at the clock. "Seven-fifteen."

"Oh, my gosh. It's too early to be awake." She pulled the cover up over her head.

"Come on. Let me see those beautiful eyes." Pulling the sheet back down from her head, her eyes finally appeared. "That's what I wanted to see." He leaned down and gave her a peck on the nose and then got out of bed.

"Where are you going?"

"I have to get to work." He pulled on his pants and went to the closet for a clean uniform.

"Would you like me to fix you some breakfast while you shower?" she asked.

"No, I'll grab a bite at the restaurant. Why don't you come with me for breakfast?"

"Actually, I want to sleep some more and then Mrs. Sampson has arranged for me to interview a lady at the library that knew Mrs. Murdock and her daughter."

"What about lunch?" he asked.

"I'll be back here at lunch. I want to work on my article this afternoon. You could come here and I'll fix something for you."

"I probably won't have time to drive out."

"Well, we'll just have to play it by ear for dinner tonight then." She rolled back over in bed and pulled the sheets up to her neck. "Have a good day."

Ben smiled and shook his head and he went into the bathroom to shower. When he came out twenty minutes later, Jaime had fallen fast asleep.

* * * *

"Morning, Angie," Ben greeted the dispatcher when he walked into the Sheriff's Department.

"Good morning, Sheriff. Here's last night's activity report and I just made a fresh pot of coffee." She motioned toward the coffee maker on the other side of the radio console.

"Thanks. I could sure use some right now." He walked over and poured himself a cup. "Is Stokes here yet?"

"I'm right here," Deputy Stokes announced, walking in for his shift. He followed Ben into his office.

Ben didn't bother sitting down while glancing at the activity log he had been given.

"So, what's on the agenda for today?" Stokes asked.

Ben looked up from the paper. "Can you go to the elementary school this morning and do that 'Don't take Candy from Strangers talk?' It's for Miss Gillespie's third grade class."

"Sure, be glad to do it." He started to walk out of the office.

"Want to go get some breakfast first?" Ben asked.

"Yeah, I could eat something."

Ben walked out of the office with Stokes following. "Angie, we'll be at the Café for breakfast, if you need us."

The two officers drove over to the Corner Café in separate cars. When they entered the restaurant, they took the table near the door.

Jenny immediately brought them both a cup of coffee. "Do you gentlemen need to see a menu?"

"No, thanks. I want a couple scrambled eggs with bacon on the side and some hash browns," Stokes said.

"That sounds good. I'll have the same," Ben added, taking a drink of his coffee.

"Thanks. I'll bring it right out." She turned and headed to the kitchen with their orders.

"Is that writer lady about finished with her snooping?" Stokes asked.

"Her name is Jaime and she has a little more to do before she's done."

"Sorry, I forgot her name. Do you have any idea who ransacked her cabin out at the lake?"

"No idea. I doubt we'll ever know. Just someone wanting to cause trouble, I suppose."

Jenny walked up with a pot of coffee. "Let me freshen up your coffee?" she asked.

"Thanks." Stokes smiled at the waitress.

Ben nodded his approval to her and couldn't help noticing Jenny and Stokes smiling at each other.

"Your breakfast should be right out," she said, walking away.

"Is there something going on between you two?" Ben asked.

"We've gone out a couple times. She's a nice girl and a lot of fun to be with."

A few minutes later, Jenny came back to the table with their food. "Here you go," setting a plate of food in front of both of them. "Can I get you anything else?" she asked, pulling a bottle of catsup out of her apron pocket and setting it on the table.

"Nothing, thanks," Ben answered.

"I'm fine, too," Stokes added.

Jenny smiled and walked away.

As the two officers enjoyed their breakfast, four older women came in and sat at the table next to them.

"Good morning, Sheriff, Deputy," one of the ladies whaled as they sat at the next table.

Ben swallowed. "Morning, ladies.

Jenny brought over the coffee pot and filled the cups sitting in front of each lady. She handed them their menus and then went to another table to take an order.

"Oh, Sheriff, could you give something to that pretty little writer for me?" one of the other ladies asked, reaching into her purse.

"I'd be glad to, Martha," he answered.

"She was telling Helen, Barb, and I at the grocery store yesterday that she was thinking of settling down here and wanted to look at some real estate," Martha winked at Ben. "Well, you know how my daughter-in-law is in the real estate business, so I stopped by her house last night and picked up some brochures about some houses in the area." She handed Ben several real estate brochures. "You two make such a nice couple."

Ben felt the heat rising in him. "Thank you, Martha. I'll see that Jaime gets these." He looked over at Deputy Stokes who was grinning from ear to ear.

"I've got work to do," Ben grumbled. He put a ten-dollar bill down on the table. "Tell Jenny to keep the change and don't forget about going to the school."

"I'll head that way in a few minutes," Stokes replied.

Ben stood up. "Ladies, it's always nice seeing your bright, cheerful faces. Have a nice day."

"You, too, Sheriff," the ladies responded.

Ben hoped he would have a good day, but it didn't look like it was going to turn out that way. He got in his patrol car and threw the stack of real estate papers on the seat.

*What the hell was she thinking by telling the town gossips that story? He started the car. Or, was it a story? Maybe Jaime really did have plans like that. She wouldn't know that those ladies spread news like wild fire.*

He felt his blood boiling again, but knew he shouldn't face her until he calmed down. He looked at his watch: nine-o'clock. He had a meeting with the Prosecutor soon, so he pulled the car out onto the street and headed to the courthouse.

* * * *

"Hi, Gabby," Jaime chirped over the cell phone to her friend. "I didn't catch you at a bad time, did I?"

"No, not at all. I'm walking to work this morning."

"And, you're doing it without me there to remind you? Fantastic." Both ladies laughed.

"So, what's up?" Gabby asked.

"Right now, I am on my way to interview someone for my article."

"That doesn't seem noteworthy of a call at eight-thirty in the morning. What's really going on, Sweetie?"

"How's Jonathan coming with his story?" Jaime deflected.

"He says he's close to finishing it. Just one more interview to do, but he still won't tell anyone what it's about. Jaime, when are you coming back?"

"I'm not sure. I still have some research to do."

She came to a stop sign and slowed her car until she stopped moving. "Gabby, I think I have fallen for the local sheriff."

"Oh, my gosh! What's going on out there?"

Suddenly, a car horn blew from behind her and Jaime started moving down the road again. "It just happened. I can't explain it."

"Jaime, you can't stay there forever. What are you going to do when you're finished there? Your job is in New York. You can't give up your career to live in Hooterville."

"I know." She turned onto the street for the Library and pulled to a stop in front. "I have to go. I'm at the Library for my interview. I'll call again soon."

"Call me tonight. We'll have a long talk over some Chamomile tea. Okay?"

"I can't."

"What do you mean, you can't?" Gabby asked.

After a hesitation, Jaime explained. "I'm staying at Ben's house and there's no privacy to talk."

"You're living with him!"

"I have to go. Bye." She quickly turned off her cell phone before Gabby could call her back. A long talk over Chamomile tea sounded so good, but it wouldn't be possible unless Ben worked late. *I need to remember to stop by the store to get some tea.*

Jaime walked into the library and was greeted by Annie Sampson. "Good morning, Jaime. How are you today?"

"I'm just fine. How are you today?"

"I couldn't be better on this beautiful fall morning."

"Has the person arrived yet that I'm to interview?"

"Yes, she's in the kitchen fixing some tea. You can talk to her in there. Come, I'll take you to her."

Jaime followed the older woman to the back of the old home converted into a library. In the kitchen, standing in front of the stove was a petite gray-haired woman.

"Eleanor, this is the young lady I wanted you to meet," Mrs. Sampson explained.

The woman turned to Jaime, who immediately noticed the wrinkled and worn face of a woman who undoubtedly spent many years working hard. She walked over to Jaime and extended her hand. "I'm Eleanor Cook and I'm pleased to meet you."

*Jackpot*, she thought, recognizing the Cook family name. "Hello, I'm Jaime Wilson from New York."

At that moment, the teapot on the stove began to whistle. "Would you like some tea, Jaime?" Mrs. Cook asked. "I brought Annie some homemade cookies today. I don't think she would mind us taking a few."

"You go right ahead and eat all you want. I'll leave you both to your visit." She turned and left, closing the door behind her.

Eleanor looked at Jaime. "Now, how about that tea?"

"I'd love some."

"I hope you like Earl Grey. It's all Annie has here at the Library."

"I love Earl Grey," she replied. Taking a seat at the table, she brought out her pad of paper, blue gel pen, and digital recorder.

Eleanor carried two cups of hot tea to the table and sat them down next to the plastic container of cookies.

"Thank you." Jaime stirred in a teaspoon of sugar and carefully took a sip of the hot drink. "This is very good."

Eleanor smiled with approval. "Most young ladies don't like hot tea, especially the taste of Earl Grey."

"I learned to drink hot tea from my late grandmother. She lived in London during her younger days and brought that tradition back with her when she came home. When I was little, we used to have tea parties."

"That's a wonderful memory to have. It's a tradition you can continue with your own children," Eleanor suggested.

"I hope to do that someday." She set her cup down. Reporter mode. "Mrs. Cook, I'd like to start the interview and will be recording it to make sure I have all the information correct for my article, if that is okay?"

"Certainly, my dear. Anything you want, but you have to call me, Eleanor."

"Okay, Eleanor it is." Jaime turned on the recorder. "What do you remember about the Murdock family?"

"It was such a tragedy when that poor family disappeared out of the blue like that."

"You were their neighbor. Is that correct?"

"Yes."

Jaime jotted down a few notes as Eleanor continued.

"I was a young housewife and mother back then..."

Thankfully, Jaime had her recorder on because her mind began wondering back to the previous night she had spent in Ben's bed. She had never been touched by a man the way Ben had touched her.

She shook her head out of the daydream realizing Eleanor was trying to get her attention.

"Jaime, is something wrong?"

"What? Oh, no. I'm fine." She readjusted herself in the chair. "I was visualizing your story in my head." *Liar.* "Please go on."

"As I was saying, I lived south of the Murdock farm, but Jacob Katt lived north of them and he and Tom Murdock didn't get along at all."

"Why is that?"

Eleanor got up to make herself another cup of tea and Jaime took a bite of a cookie.

"Jacob was older than Tom, but he took a fancy to Tom's daughter, Bonnie."

"How old was Bonnie?" Jaime asked.

"She was about twenty-one, I think. But, she was a might slow. She didn't have all of her wits about her, if you know what I mean."

"I think I understand." She wrote down Jacob Katt's name.

Eleanor came back to the table with her freshly made tea. "Would you like another cup?"

"No, thank you. Not yet. Tell me about the day they disappeared. I understand there were no bodies found in the house," Jaime inquired.

"That's right."

"What do you think happened to them?"

Eleanor hesitated. "I don't know. There are lots of theories. With Tom not working, he owed a lot of people money. Some think a creditor ran the family out of town, others think the family skipped out in the middle of the night."

"You don't think either of those things happened, do you?"

Leaning over, Eleanor whispered, "The night before they disappeared, I heard an explosion over that way."

"What kind of explosion?"

"Dynamite," Eleanor stated.

"How do you know it was dynamite?"

Eleanor straightened back up in her chair. "Once you hear dynamite explode, you recognize it every time."

"And, you had heard that sound before?"

"Plenty of times. My family owned the rock quarry that was about three miles west as the crow flies from my house back then. I heard blasting all the time."

Jaime took the last drink of her tea. "Do you have any idea what blew up that night?"

"I used to take walks in the woods back then. The weekend after the explosion, I found where a bunch of rock had been blown off a cliff."

"Had someone from the quarry done that?" Jaime asked.

"No, it was too far away from there."

"Did you report the explosion to the police?"

"Heavens no. What for?"

"Eleanor, it could have had something to do with the Murdock's disappearance."

"You know, I never thought of that."

"I'd like to see the spot where the explosion happened."

"Oh, honey. There's no way I could walk out there at my age." She got up and went to the sink to wash her cup.

Jaime turned the digital recorder off and did the same. "You could give me directions," she suggested.

"That was thirty years ago, my dear. I'm sure it's so grown up with trees and brush that you'd never find it. Besides, if you're not familiar with the woods around here, you'd likely get lost and never be found."

She wondered if Eleanor was making a joke, or telling the truth. Either way, she had to get back to that property, but the pending trespassing charges kept creeping back into her mind. She was completely blocked unless she could come up with another way.

"I really want to thank you for letting me interview you today."

"You're welcome. I've enjoyed your company," Eleanor replied, putting the lid back on the cookie container.

"I especially liked having tea with you. Do you know where I can go to buy some? The only tea I brought with me from New York is Chamomile."

"The grocery store in town is out. I stopped yesterday and bought the last box and they told me they wouldn't get any more in until next week. I'm sure the supermarket in Whitley has some, but that's thirty miles away," Eleanor reported. "Why don't you stop by my house this afternoon and I'll give you a few bags."

"That's kind of you to offer." Jaime started packing her things in a bag. "But, I'm afraid I can't step foot on your property. I have trespassing charges on me from when I first arrived in the area."

"That was you?"

"Allegedly." Jaime tried to make light of the situation. "I wanted to see the Murdock's farm."

"I'm sorry about that. My son, Malcolm, did that." Eleanor put on her sweater. "Maybe I could drop off the tea at the Sheriff's office. I hear you two are friendly."

*News travels fast around here.* "I'm sure that would be fine. Thank you."

Both ladies gathered their things and walked out in to the Library. Annie sat at the counter scanning bar codes on the stack of books in front of her.

"Will I see you tonight at Bible Study, Annie?" Eleanor asked.

"I'll be there," Annie replied. "I'm hoping you two left enough of those cookies for me to bring tonight."

"We left plenty," Eleanor informed.

"Thank you for letting us use the kitchen," Jaime related.

"Have a good day, ladies." Annie gave the ladies a little wave as they walked out the front door.

\* \* \* \*

That same evening, Ben entered the front door of his house to the smell of supper lingering in the air. Whatever she had cooked smelled wonderful to him. Nevertheless, he had to have a talk with her about what the ladies in town said today. "Jaime."

"I'm in the kitchen."

He walked in and found her at the table typing on her laptop. "We need to talk."

"What about?" she asked, not looking up from her computer.

"These." He threw the real estate booklets down on top of her keyboard.

"Hey! What did you do that for?" She looked at the booklets.

"Did you tell the town gossips yesterday that you were moving here and that we ..."

"I-I-I may have given that impression," she replied, cutting off his sentence. "But, I just said that because they were being so nosey."

"Of course they were being nosey, they're the town gossips." He turned his back to her and walked to the other side of the room.

"How did I know they would spread that around?" she retorted.

He turned back toward her. "They're gossips, Jaime. That's what they do. Martha gave me those booklets from her daughter-in-law this morning at the restaurant. My guess is that by now, they probably have the church reserved for our wedding!"

"Ben, I am so sorry. I had no idea it would escalate like this."

He stood at the kitchen window looking out. "This was a mistake. I think you need to leave."

"What?" Jaime got up and walked over to him. "You're not serious."

He turned his head and looked at her. "I called and reserved you a room at the Riverbend Bed and Breakfast in Jackson. It's a few miles past the interstate. It's quiet there and you should be able to get your article finished and back to New York in no time."

She didn't say a word, just turned and walked out of the kitchen and went to her bedroom.

Twenty minutes later, she walked into the living room carrying her suitcase and laptop bag. Her eyes looked swollen and red, no doubt from crying. "In case you didn't notice, your supper is on the stove. It's meatloaf and mashed potatoes. You told me that was your favorite." That being said, she walked out the door.

* * * *

Later, Ben found himself sitting at the kitchen table, picking at the dinner she had made. *Maybe he shouldn't have told her to leave*, he thought, handing Jake a piece of meatloaf. No, it had to be done. A relationship between them would have never worked.

Thirty minutes after supper, he sat on the couch with Jake curled up on the floor at this feet. Ben picked up the phone and dialed the number for the Riverbend Bed and Breakfast. "Mr. Andrews, this is Sheriff Hunter. Did my friend, Miss Wilson get checked in?"

"Yes, she did," the innkeeper replied. "She indicated that she wanted to be left alone though."

"That's fine. I just wanted to make sure she arrived safely. Thank you." He hung up the phone and looked at his dog. "What am I going to do, Jake?"

# Chapter Seven

After a restless sleep, Jaime woke up the next morning feeling numb after what had occurred the night before. She looked at the clock and it showed eleven o'clock. Breakfast at the Inn had long passed and her stomach pangs told her she needed food.

She threw on a sweater and jeans and walked downstairs. The desk clerk looked up from his duties.

"Good morning, Miss Wilson. Did you have a restful night?" he asked.

"Not really." Then, she noticed the confused look on his face. "No, nothing to do with the room. I have a lot on my mind and just couldn't sleep."

The clerk nodded.

"I'm sure I've missed breakfast, can you tell me where I can find the nearest restaurant?" she asked.

"There's a pretty good place out at the interstate."

"I'm familiar with it." She remembered having coffee with Ben there when she first arrived in town. "Thank you."

Jaime walked outside into the autumn air. Riverview Bed and Breakfast; the name fit. The two-story vintage house sat on a bluff overlooking a bend in the river. The deep red, yellow, and orange colors were breathtaking in the sunshine. She took a deep breath, taking in the cool crisp air. *You can't do that in New York City,* she thought. With the day being so nice, she drove to the restaurant with her window down a little.

When she entered the restaurant, she spotted a familiar face. Deputy Mark Stokes sat alone at a booth in the corner. He nodded a greeting to her and she walked over.

"Good morning, Miss Wilson," he spoke as he stood up.

"Good morning. Please, sit down. Eating alone this morning?" she asked. The last thing she wanted was to run into Ben.

"Yes, ma'am. It looks that way."

"Would you like to join me?" the deputy asked.

"Are you sure? You might be the topic of the next town gossip if I do?"

"It wouldn't be the first time."

"Nor I."

As she sat down, the waitress came over with a pot of coffee and a cup. "Coffee?"

"Yes, please," Jaime answered.

The waitress poured her a cup. "Would you like to see a menu?"

"I suppose I should. Are you still serving breakfast?"

"Bring her the Breakfast Special, Jeri," Stokes suggested. "You can wait and bring mine at the same time."

The waitress re-filled the deputy's coffee cup and headed back to the kitchen.

"What's the Breakfast Special?" Jaime asked Stokes.

"That would be eggs, bacon, hash browns and toast," he replied.

"That sounds really good."

"It is." He took a drink of his coffee and leaned forward. "So the town gossips got you, eh?"

She nodded in agreement as she swallowed a sip of coffee. "Apparently, they told the sheriff something I had said to them that I meant as a joke."

Stokes laughed. "Guess the joke was on you. I was with him when they pounced."

"Was it that bad?"

"Yeah, it was. You have to understand small towns. Everyone knows everyone else's business, or at least they think they should."

"But, why me?"

"You're new in town and everyone wants to know what the big city writer is doing here. But, it's not just you. You've taken up with the sheriff; the most eligible bachelor in the county, who all the grandmothers want their granddaughters to marry."

"Well, that's no longer the case. Ben blames me for the gossip and moved me to the Bed and Breakfast. All I want to do now is finish my article and get back to New York."

The waitress brought their food to the table and set the plates in front of them. "Here you go, two Specials. Can I bring you anything else? More coffee?"

"I'm fine," Stokes responded.

"Me, too. Thanks."

The waitress set a bottle of catsup on the table and walked away.

"How's your article going?" he asked, taking a bite of egg.

"Actually, I'm not even close to finishing it. I was hoping to be able to solve the mystery by figuring out what happened to the family." Jaime took a bite of the sandwich she had made with her eggs, bacon, and toast.

"No one has been able to figure that out after thirty years and you really think you can do it?"

She swallowed before answering. "I'm hoping I still can. I want to go back out to the Cook's farm and look around out in the woods." As soon as the words left her mouth, she knew she shouldn't have said it.

"You have to be kidding. You want to go back out there after being arrested once already?"

"No. No. I meant I wish I could go back out there." She hoped he wouldn't tell Ben about her plans.

"Exactly how do you plan on solving these alleged murders?" he asked, sounding more like a police officer.

She took a sip of her coffee. "I'm not here to solve anything. I just want to write the story."

The waitress came back placing their checks on the table. "Will there be anything else?"

"Thanks, Jeri. I think we're good." Stokes flashed her a smile.

"Something going on between you and the waitress?" Jaime asked.

"Jeri? No, we're just friends." He blushed.

"You're a real player, aren't you, Deputy Stokes? If you came to New York with that 'Aw shucks' personality, the ladies would eat you up."

His face turned as red as a cherry Mustang.

Jaime quickly snatched up both checks. "I'll take care of these."

"I can't let you do that."

"Nonsense. I can turn these in as an expense. It won't cost me a cent." She pulled a credit card out of her purse.

"At least let me get the tip," he suggested.

"Okay, you take care of that. I should get going. I have an interview to do." She lied, knowing full well she planned on driving to the Cook's farm. "Thanks for having breakfast with me."

The temperature had warmed even more since going into the restaurant, so she drove with her window all the way down to enjoy the fresh air. By the time she arrived at the farm, her car clock showed one o'clock.

Slowly, she drove up the driveway and parked next to the barn. Then, grabbing her backpack, she walked behind the barn and noticed a worn path leading into the woods. She studied the topographical map she had copied at the library. This had to be the trail to the cliff area Eleanor had mentioned.

Before heading down the trail, Jaime snapped a couple photos of the area. After walking for about a hundred yards, the trail came to fork.

It looked like the main trail went to the left then led to a clearing of some sort a little way down, so she headed that way.

Reaching the small clearing, she found three old gravestones. No names, no dates, just plain markers.

She snapped pictures of all three headstones and as she put her camera away, she heard a stick snap behind her. Quickly, she twisting around and found Ben towering over her.

"Being arrested once wasn't enough?" he asked, turning her around and handcuffing her hands behind her back.

"Ben, wait. You're making a mistake. I can explain."

"I don't want to hear it." He picked up her backpack and grabbed her by the arm to march her out.

"Will you let me explain?"

"You're under arrest, *again,* for trespassing. I hope you liked our jail last time because you'll be spending the night there this time."

"Why won't you listen to me?" she pleaded.

"I told you to stop talking. If you say another word, I'm going to gag you."

He sounded as though he meant it, so Jaime didn't say anything else.

When they got back to the farm they found Malcolm Cook leaning against Ben's police car. "Nice job, Sheriff," he whaled.

Just as Ben was about to put Jaime into the backseat, a female voice called out from the porch of the house.

Jaime immediately recognized the voice and turned to see Eleanor rushing to them as fast as her frail body would allow.

"What are you doing, Sheriff?" Take those things off of her right now," Eleanor demanded.

"Mother, she's trespassing again. The sheriff is only doing his job."

"She's doing no such thing. I told the prosecutor to drop the trespassing charge, and I told Jaime she could come out here anytime she wanted." She then turned to Ben. "Now, take those things off of her."

"Yes, ma'am."

"Wait a minute, Sheriff. Mother, you can't drop that charge. You aren't the one that filed it. I did."

"But, your name isn't on the deed. I own this property and when I told the prosecutor that, he told me that legally you didn't have the authority to file the charge. So, they were dropped."

Malcolm put his hands on his hips and looked disgusted. Finally, he turned, got into his car and sped off.

Eleanor looked at Ben. "Sheriff?"

Ben removed the handcuffs from Jaime's wrists.

"I tried to tell you," she muttered, alternately rubbing her wrists.

He shook his head. "What were you doing out there anyway?"

Jaime looked at the older lady who gave her an approving nod. "Eleanor told me about a place where it looked like someone had blown the side of the cliff off. She found it not long after the Murdock family had disappeared. I wanted to see if I could find it. Now, if you don't mind, I'm going back out there."

"Let me get my cane off the porch. I want to go with you." Eleanor quickly headed back to the porch.

Jaime leaned toward Ben and whispered, "Yesterday, she told me she didn't think she could walk all the way back there."

"Mrs. Cook," Ben called after her. "I'm not sure if it's a good idea for you to walk that far out in the woods."

Eleanor retrieved her cane and had almost returned back to where Jaime and Ben waited when she answered. "Nonsense. I used to walk over that whole hillside when I went mushroom hunting."

"Mushroom hunting?" Jaime questioned.

"Yes, each spring Morel mushrooms pop up in the woods. Best food you can fry," Eleanor replied. "Come on, let's get going while we have daylight."

"I'm going with you, too," Ben insisted.

"Why?" Jaime asked.

He nodded his head toward Eleanor "If she should fall, you'll need help getting her up."

The three of them walked slowly along the trail until they reached the fork. "The graves I found are this way," Jaime told Eleanor.

A few minutes later, they stood over the markers.

"Do either of you have any idea who's buried here?" Jaime asked.

"I've never seen these before," Ben replied.

"This must be the place where some old Indian bones were reburied."

"Indians didn't bury their dead with markers like these."

"These were the bones that Malcolm and a couple of his friends found about eight months after the Murdock's disappeared. Some doctor in Indiana University confirmed that they were Indian bones.

They were reburied here. My husband told them they could bury them here since it was close to where they were found."

"Were you here when they were buried?" Jaime asked.

"No honey, I wasn't. I was in the hospital recovering from gall bladder surgery."

"Let's walk to the cliff," Jaime suggested. "I want to see it."

The trio took off with Eleanor leading. Jaime pulled at Ben's arm to hold him back, letting Eleanor get several steps ahead of them.

"Do you believe that story?" she asked.

"About the Indian bones? It could be true."

"I'm going to check the newspaper archives again to see what I can find about it."

"You kids a comin'?" Eleanor shouted back to them.

"On our way," Jaime replied.

The walk to the cliffs took a little longer with Eleanor's slow pace, but finally they reached it. Jaime peered over the edge and saw thirty years of tree and vegetative growth over some huge boulders.

"This is it. This is where I found the rocks blown from the hillside." Eleanor took a step closer.

"Don't get too close to the edge, Mrs. Cook," Ben cautioned. "The weathered sandstone could break loose at any time."

"I want to go down there," Jaime announced.

"You've got to be kidding. It must be thirty or forty feet down," he exclaimed. "It's too dangerous."

"You could walk in from the road down below my house," Eleanor said.

Jaime turned to Ben. "Could you walk in with me?"

Before he could answer, his radio sounded a tone and the dispatcher called him. "Six-Oh-One, Butler County."

"This is Six-Oh-One," he answered into his radio.

"Six-Oh-One, we have a multi-car accident with injuries on the interstate at the thirty mile marker. Your assistance is being requested by a state unit to help with traffic control."

"Roger. ETA will be about thirty minutes."

"Affirmative, Six-Oh-One. Clear."

"Don't wait on me, Sheriff. Jaime and I can make it back just fine by ourselves."

Ben looked at Jaime. "Don't let anything happen to her."

"I won't, sir," Jaime saluted, mocking a soldier at attention.

He moved closer to her. So close, she could feel his hot breath against her face. "I'm serious. If anything happens to her, Malcolm will see to it that you're locked up for a long time."

"I understand," she quietly replied, stepping back.

"Mrs. Cook, be careful on the walk back." He then turned to Jaime and pointed his finger at her. "Don't go down that cliff or anywhere in the ravine by yourself."

"I won't."

Ben took off trotting down the trail back toward the farm.

"You two make a lovely couple," Eleanor commented.

Jaime let out a deep breath. "Oh, we're not a couple."

"That's too bad."

On the walk back to the house, Eleanor had to make a few stops to rest. "Let's stop here by this boulder for a few minutes and then I think I'll be able to make it the rest of the way." She and Jaime both shared a large boulder. "You know my husband used to walk all over these woods when he went squirrel hunting. He told Malcolm and me that he had always heard that there was an old lead mine back here somewhere."

"Did he ever find it?"

"No, I don't think so. If he had, I'd be a rich woman now." Both ladies laughed. "I think I'm ready to go now."

A short time later, they came out of the woods next to Eleanor's red barn.

"Come on in the house with me and I'll give you those Earl Gray tea bags I promised."

Jaime only stayed long enough to get the tea from Eleanor and then bid her good-bye. She got in her car and headed back to town. By the time she parked in front of the newspaper office, the clock at the bank showed two-thirty.

When she went inside, she found Kenneth and Sam Morgan standing in the front lobby in a heated discussion.

"I need to get back to work," Sam sneered, as soon as he saw Jaime and stomped back to his office.

Kenneth greeted her. "It's good to see you again, Miss Wilson. What brings you back to our office?"

"Please, call me Jaime and I'd like to look through your archives again, if I could."

"Of course, you can. Come this way, I'll walk you to the door. I've got to get back to my office to give the final approval for tomorrow's edition." They walked together down the hallway.

"I appreciate you giving me access like this. It has really been helpful with the background part of my article."

"How is your story coming?"

"Not bad. I still have a lot of work to do on it though."

"What are you researching today?" he asked.

Jaime hesitated before answering. She hated letting anyone know about leads she was chasing and visualized being scooped on the front page of the local newspaper.

Deciding he might have some info she could use, she reluctantly gave in. "I discovered some graves in the woods behind Eleanor Cook's farm. She said they were from a reburial of Indian bones found about thirty years ago."

"You think the Murdock family is buried in those graves?" He laughed. "Eleanor is right. Those are some old Indian bones found around that time."

"I'd just like to see if there was anything in the newspaper about it."

They reached the basement door and Kenneth opened it and turned on the light for her. "I think you know your way around down there."

"I remember. Thanks. I won't be too long."

"Best I can remember, those bones were found during squirrel season. Look in issues after August fifteen. That's always the first day of squirrel season."

"Thanks." Jaime carefully stepped down the stairs into the basement and took a seat at the microfiche reader. Thanks to Kenneth's suggestion, she soon found some articles.

One had a crude map of where the bones were found. She printed the map and the accompanying article. Another article had the names of the hunters that found the bones. "Well, isn't that interesting," she mumbled to herself. Finally, she found a story about the reburial of the bones, but no photos accompanied the article. She printed the articles and packed everything away.

She checked the clock on the wall, three-thirty, and thought there might be enough daylight left for another trip into the woods.

The rain had ended by the time she reached the Cook farm again. She knocked on Eleanor's door to tell her she was going into the woods again, but no one answered. She figured after the long walk they had earlier that Eleanor was probably napping.

Jaime left the porch and started down the trail. The rain that had already fallen on top of the leaves made it a somewhat slippery walk. She also found that the lateness of the day combined with the overcast sky made the forest much darker than she had anticipated. Thunder rumbled from the west and the rain started falling again.

"I must be insane to be out here again," she uttered.

By the time she reached the cliffs, the wind picked up and the rain steadily came down, so she raised the hood of her jacket over her head.

She peered over the edge and decided if she could just climb down on the right side a little ways, she could get under that rock overhang and out of the rain until it let up.

Jaime took one step to the right and suddenly felt something touch her back. The next thing she knew she was tumbling down toward the bottom of the ravine.

*Green*, she saw green as she fell and then lost consciousness.

# Chapter Eight

Jaime found it hard to open her eyes and fought to come out of the fog that clouded her head. Once her eyes opened, she saw a bright light and a tall figure towering over her. *I've died and gone to heaven*, she thought.

"Welcome back," a familiar voice echoed in her head. "Jaime, can you hear me?"

"Ben?" she managed to mumble.

"Yeah, it's me. How are you feeling?"

"Like I was run over by a bus." She winced in pain as she tried to sit up. "What happened and where am I?"

"Lay still. You slipped on the wet rocks and fell over the edge. You're at the hospital in Whitley, not far from Royal." Ben pushed the button to raise the head of the bed. "You have a concussion, some broken ribs, a sprained wrist, and from what they tell me, a lot of bruises."

"My mouth is so dry; can I have some water?"

Ben pushed the button for the nurse who brought ice chips instead of water. "With a concussion, we want to limit your water intake because it could make you nauseated. These ice chips should help though. I'll let the doctor know you're awake. I'll be back later to check your vitals."

She handed Ben the cup and left the room. "You want me to feed this to you?" he asked.

"No." He handed the cup of ice to her and she spooned some in her mouth. "How did I get here?"

Ben took the cup from her and sat it on the table. "Malcolm Cook saw your car at Eleanor's this morning and called me. I found you at the bottom of the cliff. You were there all night and have been unconscious since."

"What time is it?"

"A little after one. Malcolm wanted to file trespassing charges again, but I think I talked him out of it."

"I didn't think he could do that."

A worried look appeared across Ben's face. "There was an accident. Eleanor fell inside her home. When Malcolm found her, you weren't there, but your car was still in the driveway."

"Is she okay?" Jaime asked.

"The last I checked, she was still unconscious. Malcolm said the doctor told him that she hit her head and they aren't sure she will come out of it. Malcolm immediately went to the judge and had himself appointed as Eleanor's guardian."

"I don't like him at all."

"I think he feels the same way about you. Anyway, I told him you would not step foot on their property again," he voiced sternly, waving his finger at her, "and you won't either."

Jaime started to protest, but someone unexpected walked into the room carrying two cups of coffee. "Oh, my gosh, you're awake!"

"Gabby? What are you doing here?" Jaime asked.

"The sheriff here called me as soon as he got you to the hospital and I took the first flight out." She handed Ben a cup of coffee.

"Thanks. I'll leave you two ladies to yourselves. Jaime, I'll stop by in the morning to check on you." He exited the room.

"Bye, Ben. Thank you." Jaime then turned her attention back to Gabby. "You didn't have to come here."

"Yes, I did. When Ben called, he implied you were hurt pretty bad. I wasn't going to let you wake up in a hospital full of strangers. Although, waking up to Sheriff Ben Hunter certainly wasn't bad, was it?"

"Things have changed a little since I last spoke with you. I'm not staying at Ben's house anymore. He asked me to leave." Jaime tried reaching for the cup of ice chips. Gabby placed it on the bedside table and rolled it next to her.

"He may have asked you to leave, but he has been wearing a hole through the floor from pacing while waiting for you to wake up."

"Really?"

"He even sent a deputy to pick me up at the airport. He's such a sweet guy."

"Do you know when I can leave?" Jaime asked.

"I'm sure you'll have to stay at least for tonight and then see what the doctor says in the morning."

"I have to get back to my article investigation."

"You're going to have to take it easy for a while, sweetie."

"This town is hiding something about that missing family."

"What makes you think that?"

"Gabby, I didn't fall off that cliff. I was pushed."

* * * *

Bright and early the next morning, Jaime kept an eye on the doorway of her room, waiting for the doctor to walk in. Sounds filled the hospital corridor, but she thought she could hear the sound of hard-soled shoes coming her way. Instead of the doctor, the footsteps belonged to a police officer. Ben, dressed in full uniform, stepped inside.

He looked as good today in the dark brown shirt and light brown pants as he did the first time she saw him. The squeak of his leather belt still sent a shiver up her spine.

"Good morning," He placed the small vase of flowers he brought by the window. "I thought you might like these."

"Thank you. They're lovely."

"How are you feeling today?"

Before she could answer, Gabby popped into the room all bouncy and cheerful. "Morning, Flash. How are you feel—Oh, sorry, I didn't know you had a visitor."

"Good morning, Gabrielle."

"Good morning to you, Sheriff. But, please call me Gabby." She took a sip from the Starbuck's cup she held. "So, how are you today?" she asked Jaime.

"I'm good, but I could be much better if you'd hand me that coffee."

"Sorry, sweetie. No caffeine until it's cleared by the doctor."

"Am I being talked about in here?" a silver-haired man stepped into the room and then introduced himself to Jaime. "I'm Dr. Summers. I saw you when you came in to the ER yesterday."

"I should probably go." Ben started toward the door.

"No, wait. Don't go yet. I need to talk to you about something," Jaime called. Ben stopped and moved over by the window.

"So, Dr. Summers, can I get out of here today?" Jaime asked.

He looked over her chart he had carried in with him. "Do you know how lucky you are, Miss Wilson? I understand you fell about forty feet."

"And, I think I hit every rock on the way down," she replied.

He looked up from the chart and laid it on the table. As he checked her eyes with a small light, he questioned her. "Do you have a headache right now?"

"It doesn't feel like a regular headache, but just a dull pain."

He then felt for the bump on her head. "I believe the swelling is going down a bit." He then checked her wrist. "How do you feel overall?"

"I'm sore all over and, other than that dull pain in my head, I feel fine. Can I get out of here?"

"I want another MRI of your head first. If it doesn't look any worse and if there is no bleeding or swelling, you should be able to go home by this evening. But, with restrictions."

"We'll make sure she follows your orders once she's released," Gabby assured him.

"Good. I'll get your MRI scheduled for later today." Dr. Summers turned to leave.

"Can I have some coffee?" Jaime asked.

The doctor turned slightly. "Decaf only, for now."

"I might as well stick with water," Jaime complained after he left the room.

Ben stepped closer to the bed. "I need to get to work. What did you want to talk to me about?"

She motioned for Gabby to close the door. Then started explaining. "Someone in Royal doesn't want me investigating the Murdock's disappearance."

"You're just now figuring that out? You did take a hard hit to the head," he teased.

"Of course I've known that for a while, but this is different. Ben, someone pushed me over the edge of that cliff."

"What? Are you sure?"

"I think I felt a hand on my back before going over the edge and as I was falling, I remember seeing something green, like a rain jacket."

"Did you hear anyone come up behind you?" he asked.

"No, but it was raining, and the ground was soaked. I didn't make much noise myself as I walked out there. If someone were trying to sneak up on me, they could have done it fairly easy."

"What shade of green did you see?"

"I don't know, just green. Not bright, not dark, sort of medium green."

"Where on your back did you feel him touch you?"

"This sounds like an interrogation."

"It's just routine questions for now. Tell me, where did you feel the push?"

"In the middle of my back, between my shoulder blades." She leaned forward and reached behind herself to try and show him. Ben moved closer to the bed and touched the middle of her back.

"Here?"

"Yes, right around there," she replied.

Ben looked down toward the floor and shook his head and sat down in the chair next to her bed.

"You don't believe me, do you? You think I'm imagining things because of my head injury."

"No. On the contrary, I do believe you. I believe you enough that when you leave the hospital, I want both you and Gabby to stay back to my house. It'll be much safer for you there than at the bed & breakfast."

Before Jaime could protest, Gabby spoke up. "I think that's a great idea. I can go ahead and pack your things for you today."

"I suppose that would be best, but only until I am feeling better," Jaime sighed and then looked at Ben. "You could ask Eleanor if she saw anyone. Maybe she saw something suspicious around her house while I was in the woods."

Ben's expression immediately changed. "Eleanor has not regained consciousness. She's been moved to a nursing home."

"Oh no." Jaime couldn't believe what he had just told her.

"Malcolm said there's still a small chance she could come out of it."

Jaime read optimism all over his face, but knew what he really meant. "Don't you think it's more than a coincidence that both Eleanor and I had such serious accidents so close in both time and place?"

"You think the same person is responsible for both of your accidents?" Gabby asked.

"Sure. It only makes sense. We were both hurt around the same time; her in her house and me out in her woods."

"I suppose you have a suspect?" Ben asked.

"I think Malcolm did it and I think he's involved in the Murdock's disappearance."

"What?" Ben laughed. "What kind of medication do they have you on?"

"I'm serious, and I have proof."

"What kind of proof?" he asked.

"I don't have it here. It's in my room at the B & B, with my research. When I get out of here today...."

"*If* you get out of here today," Ben interrupted.

She then repeated herself, "*When* I get out of here today, I'll show you at your house tonight."

"Okay, tonight then." He got up and started toward the door. "I have to get to work."

"Ben, where's my backpack that I had with me?" Jaime asked.

"It's in the truck of my police car."

"Good. Keep it safe for me, okay?"

"I will. Call me *if* they say you can leave today. I'll come pick you up."

"*When* they say I can leave, I'll call."

He just shook his head as he opened the door and left the room.

"I told you he was still interested in you," Gabby teased, as soon as he was out of her ear-shot.

"Maybe. I like him, but he lives here and I don't think a long-distance relationship would work."

"Has he told you much about himself?"

"A little. He grew up here, left for college, worked for a while in Chicago and then moved back here and was elected sheriff. Why?"

Gabby moved to the chair that Ben had just vacated. "Please don't be mad at me, but when you told me you were becoming involved with him, I checked him out."

"No, I'm not mad, I don't think. How did you do that?"

"I have a friend that works at the *Chicago Tribune*. He checked their database for anything on Ben."

"And, your friend found something?" Jaime held her breath waiting for the answer.

"He did. Oh, don't worry, it's not anything bad."

"So, what did he find?"

"Apparently, after Ben got out of college, he went to work as Head of Security in a big hotel in Chicago."

"That's what he told me."

Suddenly, the ladies heard a knock at the door and before Jaime could say anything, a nurse's aide came in carrying a tray. "Dr. Summers approved you a light breakfast and decaf coffee."

She placed the tray on the bedside table and moved it over for Jaime to eat.

"Thank you. Could you close the door on your way out?" Jaime asked.

After the door closed, Gabby continued. "Ben became involved with a female security guard that worked at the hotel. She eventually became his girlfriend."

"That wasn't very professional of him." Jaime took the lid off of the coffee and took a drink.

"Apparently, he and his girlfriend thought the same thing because she requested and was granted a transfer to the office staff."

"Did something happen?" Jaime asked.

"On her last night with the Security Department before her transfer, she happened upon a robbery in the parking garage. She was shot and killed."

"Oh, my gosh."

"My friend was the reporter who covered the story and he said Ben blamed himself for her death because he assigned her to that shift."

"He must have been devastated."

"So much that he moved back here as soon as the investigation was completed."

"And, he buried himself in his work. No wonder he doesn't want to date anyone around here."

"Except for you."

"I don't know. I was convenient, the out-of-towner he could sleep with and have no commitment." Jaime took a bite of toast.

"I think you're wrong about that. You didn't see the concern on his face while we waited for you to wake up."

Jaime started to protest, but the door opened again and a nurse walked in pushing a machine on wheels.

"Good morning, Miss Wilson. I'm here to take your vitals this morning."

Quickly, the nurse took her blood pressure, pulse, and temperature. "Everything looks pretty good. You're scheduled for a MRI in about an hour and if the results are normal, then you should be discharged later this evening."

"I think I had better go and get you checked out of the inn. I'll be back later and we can call Ben to meet us here when you're discharged."

That afternoon, Jaime called both Ben and Gabby to tell them the MRI was fine and she could leave after four o'clock.

Right on time, Ben walked into her hospital room where Gabby, who had already arrived, sat talking with Jaime.

"Good afternoon, ladies." He looked at Jaime. "Are you ready to get out of this place?"

"I sure am. I just need to ring for the nurse."

She pushed the button on the bedside and a voice came over the speaker. "Yes, Miss Wilson."

"I'm ready to leave now."

"Someone will be right there with your discharge paperwork and a wheelchair."

A few minutes later, the nurse came in the room with an aide behind her, pushing a wheelchair.

"I bet you can't wait to leave," the nurse commented.

"I am ready. Thank you and your staff for such good care."

"You're welcome. Now, I have a few things for you to sign." She showed Jaime where to sign on each page.

"Okay."

"This last one is your Discharge Orders." The nurse began reading them to Jaime. "You should not be left alone. Have a friend stay with you for about a week."

"That's not a problem. I have these two to watch over me." She motioned toward Gabby and Ben.

"Initially, you should be on a light diet and gradually advance your diet back to normal. Do not drink any alcoholic beverages for at least a week."

"What about caffeine?" Jaime interrupted. "I really need my coffee."

"You can have coffee, but it still needs to be decaffeinated."

Jaime looked at Gabby and Ben. "I guess no Starbucks yet."

The nurse smiled and continued. "Avoid strenuous activities, no lifting or straining for a week and no sex for at least a week either."

Jaime looked over at Gabby, who already had a big grin spread across her face. She didn't dare look at Ben.

"Don't drive or operate machinery. Avoid taking any medication that would make you sleepy. If you aren't sure, call Dr. Summers' office. Also, don't take any anti-inflammatory medications, such as aspirin or ibuprofen. If you have a mild headache, you can take Tylenol. If that doesn't help, call the doctor. Finally, if you have any dizziness that doesn't go away, trouble walking, or nausea, call the doctor right away. Do you understand all of these instructions?"

"Yes, I do."

The nurse handed Jaime the clipboard with the instructions for her to sign. With the paperwork completed, Jaime could leave. She took a seat on the wheelchair, Ben picked up her bag, and Gabby carried the flowers that Ben had brought her earlier.

They reached the hospital entrance. "I'll go get my car." Ben started to head to the parking lot.

"Actually, I think I'll ride with Gabby, if you don't mind."

His face blushed slightly, "Of course, I should have realized that. Turn left on the highway that runs in front of the hospital, it will take you back to Royal," he told Gabby, and then looked at Jaime. "You should know the way to my house once you get to Royal."

"I remember."

"I'll follow behind you."

"I better go get the car." Gabby hurried off to the parking lot, leaving Jaime and Ben alone, except for the nurse's aide.

The silence felt uncomfortably quiet until Jaime finally spoke. "The fall foliage certainly is pretty in this part of the country. The leaves back home in Central Park won't turn for at least a few more weeks."

"It's a good season for the leaves. It brings in a lot of tourists to look at them. You were lucky to have gotten a room at the Bed and Breakfast."

"Yeah, real lucky," she replied, remembering the circumstances that resulted in her being at the inn.

More silence continued until Gabby drove up in Jaime's rental car. Ben put her bag in the backseat and then took Jaime's hand to help her into the car.

"I'll see you at my place." He closed the car door. He then looked at Gabby, who stood next to the driver's door. "Go ahead. I'll catch up to you."

Gabby pulled the car out onto the street and, following Jaime's directions, they were soon on the highway heading toward Royal.

"Gabby, how long are you going to be able to stay?" Jaime looked at the side mirror and saw that Ben had caught up to them. Even in the reflection of the mirror, she couldn't get the thought out of her head about how sexy he looked in those dark aviator sunglasses.

"I was going to talk to you about that tonight. I can only stay a couple more days, maybe stretch it to three, but I have to be back in New York by Thursday afternoon at the latest. I have an interview scheduled with someone for an article."

"I knew you wouldn't be able to stay much longer. I'm a little worried about staying at Ben's after you leave. The situation may be uncomfortable."

"Why don't you come back with me? While I stayed in your room at the inn, I looked through the notes for your article. It looked like you've got plenty enough to finish your article."

"Turn right at the next road up there," Jaime pointed ahead of them. "I know I could finish it, but something doesn't feel right about it. There's more to it and I want to find out what. Besides, I want to know who pushed me over the cliff."

Gabby turned onto the road, narrower and curvier than the highway. "Are you sure that's the reason. The real reason?"

"You think I'm procrastinating because of Ben?" She checked the mirror again to make sure he had also turned.

"The thought had crossed my mind. Maybe you don't really want to leave here. I'm not a country person by any means, but these fall days, clean air, and quiet nights sure are appealing."

"Turn left at that mailbox. That's Ben's driveway."

Gabby parked the car next to his truck into the driveway. "That's Ben's truck, but he doesn't drive it much. He mainly uses the police car," Jaime explained.

Ben got out of his car and quickly had Jaime's door open. "Let me help you." He took her hand as she got out and when she wobbled a little, he put his hand on her back to steady her.

"Dizzy?"

"Only for a moment. Thanks," she replied.

He and Jaime led the way into the house. Gabby grabbed Jaime's bag from the backseat and followed.

"You can put my bag in the room through that door." Jaime motioned toward the room she had occupied only a few days earlier.

"No," Ben called out. "Gabrielle can stay in that room. You can sleep in my room and I'll sleep on the couch."

"I can't put you out of your own room. Gabby and I can both stay in there."

"You'll each be more comfortable in your own beds." He helped Jaime to the couch and then took the bag from Gabby, carrying it to his bedroom.

"Well, that's one way to get you back in his bed," Gabby whispered.

Ben and Gabby then carried the rest of the things in from the car while Jaime sat on the couch petting Jake, who rested his head in her lap.

"He's missed you, you know?" Ben said, after making the final trip and sitting down in the chair close to her.

"You're making that up."

"No, I swear. He's been lying in front of that bedroom door every night, like he's waiting for you to come out."

"Did you miss me, boy?" she asked, scratching behind the dog's ear. Jake gave her hand a lick and she smiled.

Gabby walked into the living room after unpacking. "I'm starved and I bet both of you are, too."

"I've got a frozen pizza that I can put in the oven," Ben suggested.

Gabby started laughing. "Frozen pizza. I think not. Point me to the kitchen and I'll see what I can throw together, if that's okay with you?"

"That's fine with me. The kitchen is at the end of the hallway on the right. Good luck finding much more than pizza though."

Gabby headed down the hall and Ben moved over to the couch closer to Jaime. Jake raised his head looking at Ben.

"She can whip up anything," Jaime said.

"Is that right?"

"Before she became a magazine writer, she went to culinary school. She's a fantastic cook."

"That's good."

The room fell silent with the only noise being the dog's breathing as he now slept at Jaime's feet.

"He's not the only one who has missed you."

"What?"

"Jake's not the only one who's missed you around here." Upon hearing his name, the dog lifted his head and looked at his owner.

"Ben."

"Let me finish. I missed you too and I'm sorry about what happened. I shouldn't have made you leave. I should have realized you were only joking with those women."

"Ben, it's okay. I understand. You were right telling me to leave. I shouldn't have made up that story I told them."

The dog got up and walked over and sat next to Ben. He reached over and petted Jake. "Ever since I've moved back to Royal, everyone has been trying to marry me off to their daughters."

"I take it there's no good prospects?" she asked.

He chuckled a little at that question. "There's plenty of pretty ladies, just none I want to spend time with."

"It must have been hard to come back here after your girlfriend's death in Chicago."

Ben's posture went straight and he looked at Jaime. "How did you know about that? No one around here knows what happened!" His eyes darted accusingly to the kitchen.

"Please don't be mad at Gabby. When I told her that I moved in here not long after arriving, she checked up on you. She was only looking out for my safety."

"That was none of her business. She shouldn't have done that, but I understand her concern for your well-being."

"Her death must have been horrible for you."

"I had a difficult time with it, but I've moved on."

"Dinner is ready," Gabby announced, as she popped into the room. They both got up and went into the kitchen, followed by Jake.

"What were you able to stir up?" Jaime asked.

Gabby brought the food to the table. "Chicken Quesadillas and Cheesy Risotto. I know one is Mexican and one is Italian, but I didn't have much to work with."

"You were able to make this from what I had here in the kitchen?" Ben asked.

"I told you she could whip up anything. This looks and smells wonderful."

"Thanks."

Jaime dug in.

"Take it easy, sweetie. You're supposed to be on a light diet to start."

"I know, but I think I can handle this. Besides, I'm starved."

"Ben, I hope you don't mine, but I poured myself a glass of wine from an open bottle I found in the refrigerator," Gabby inquired.

He looked at Jaime. "You better ask her, it's her wine."

"I should have known. It's your favorite brand."

"It's fine that you have some. You know that."

"I'm going to have a beer. I think there's a diet soda still in the there, if you want it," he asked Jaime, getting up and going to the refrigerator.

"Yes, please."

Dinner conversation kept mostly to Ben telling Gabby how great it is to live around Royal.

"Sounds great, but I think I'll stick to just visiting. I'm definitely a city girl." She rose from the table and started clearing off the dishes.

"Not me. I don't miss the city at all. I plan on living here for the rest of my life," Ben stated, carrying his dishes to the sink. "I better take Jake out for a walk. C'mon boy."

As soon as he stepped outside, the girls started talking. "I told you it wouldn't work out," Jaime reminded her.

"Long distance relationships have worked for some people." Gabby tried to encourage her.

"Not us." Jaime got up to help with the dishes. "Let's put all of these into the dishwasher."

By the time the dishwasher had been loaded and running, Ben

came back in with a very happy looking dog.

Jaime knelt down to pet him. "Isn't it amazing how they look like they're smiling?"

"He likes you. He has from the first time you came here and he doesn't take to most people so fast."

"I want to take a picture of him. Do you have my backpack?" Jaime asked.

"It's still in my car. Why don't you all go into the living room and I'll go get it."

Once in the room, Ben went outside and Gabby quickly sat in the chair, leaving only the couch for Jaime and Ben.

"I know what you're doing."

"My matchmaking skills are a little rusty, but they're coming back fast." Gabby laughed and Jake barked. "Hey, you should be on my side. I'm trying to keep them together."

"Try all you want, but you're not getting it."

"Not getting what?" Ben asked, walking back into the house carrying the backpack and handing it to Jaime.

"She was telling me that I'm not going to get that Assistant Editor job at the magazine because she wants it," Gabby slyly related.

"What the hell?" Jaime started dropping pieces of her camera on the coffee table. "Look at my camera."

"It must have broken during your fall," Ben suggested, as Jaime continued looking through her bag. "I found it lying next to you at the bottom of the cliff."

"It's gone. It's all gone." She dumped the rest of the contents of the bag onto the table. "All of that research I did after getting here is gone."

"What's gone, sweetie?" Gabby asked.

"Everything. All the articles that I printed at the newspaper office that day, they're all gone."

"Are you sure they were in your bag?" Ben asked, taking a seat on the couch.

"Yes, I printed them at the newspaper office and then went straight to the Cook's farm."

"Your bag has been in the trunk of my car ever since I found you and I have the only key. No one could have gotten to your bag in there."

Jaime examined the camera more closely. "The memory card is gone."

"What was on the card?" he asked.

"Pictures that I took of those graves and around the cliff. Someone stole the memory card and those articles."

"Why would someone take that stuff? You can retake the pictures and print the articles again," Gabby stated.

"I'll tell you why," Ben added. "If she hadn't survived the fall, no one would know about the pictures or the articles."

"And, no one finds out what really happened to the Murdock family." Jaime finished his sentence. "Now, do you believe someone pushed me over the cliff?"

"I always believed you," he assured her.

"So, what happens now?" Gabby asked.

"I need to get something from my car." Ben walked outside and in a few minutes returned with an evidence bag. He held it open in front of Jaime. "Put the camera and pieces in here. It's a long shot, but I'll have the State Police check it for fingerprints."

Jaime carefully dropped the camera and broken pieces into the clear plastic bag. Ben zipped it closed and wrote something on the bag.

"Now, it's an official investigation. I need to take this to the office and put it in the evidence locker."

"It can't wait until morning?"

"No, it has to be kept in a secure place and as much as I'd like to think my house is secure, the court doesn't agree."

Gabby yawned and stretched her arms above her head. "I'm really tired and think I'll head to bed now."

"Goodnight, Gabby."

"See you tomorrow," Ben added.

Gabby left the room, closing the bedroom door behind her.

"You're probably pretty tired, too."

"Yes. It's been a long day." She looked toward the master bedroom door.

"I need to get a pillow and a blanket out of the closest in the bedroom. I should do that now so I don't wake you later after I get back from town."

They walked into the bedroom, followed by Jake. Jaime stood nervously by the bed while Ben got the pillow and blanket. While in there, Ben also pulled a cleanly pressed brown uniform out of the closet. "I'll need this for tomorrow."

Jaime smiled back at him.

"I'll try not to be gone long and will double-check that the doors and windows are locked." As he moved toward the door, he stopped because Jake stood in the doorway. "Stay in here with her, boy."

The dog walked over next to Jaime and sat at her feet.

"I think I'll be in good hands, or should I say paws."

"Come to the Sheriff's Department in the morning and we'll go over some things about your case," he instructed, pausing for a split second before going out the door.

"Goodnight." She closed the door behind him. She wondered if he had started to kiss her goodnight when he paused, but shook that thought from her head. After changing into her pajamas and crawling under the covers, Jake jumped up on the bed and curled up at her feet. "Goodnight, Jake."

# Chapter Nine

The next morning, Jaime and Gabby walked into the Sheriff's Department hoping to find Ben available. "Good morning, Angie," Jaime said to the clerk behind the window. "Is the sheriff in?"

"He's in, but on the phone. Have a seat and I'll tell him you're here."

Jaime sat down, but Gabby walked around the room checking out all the posters and notices on the wall.

"I'm impressed," Gabby commented.

"Impressed with what?"

"I admit I came here with a preconceived conception that this would be like the Mayberry Town Hall, but it's not. It's a fully functioning professional police department."

"I wouldn't expect anything less from Ben."

Gabby had moved to a bulletin board next to the public restroom. "Oh, oh, I may have spoken too soon."

"What is it?"

"There's a flyer here for a Halloween Dance coming up, and the best costume wins a 10-speed bicycle from the hardware store. Wow."

"The costume contest is for the kids and that bulletin board is for community events, if you would have noticed," Deputy Stokes pointed out, standing at the front door.

"I'm sorry. I didn't mean..."

"She didn't mean anything by that, Mark. Truth be told, Gabby is from a town in upstate New York smaller than this one."

"Guilty," Gabby added, walking over and taking the seat next to Jaime.

"Deputy Mark Stokes, this is my best friend Gabrielle Santoro."

"It's a pleasure, Deputy. My friends call me, Gabby." She stood up and extended her hand, flashing him a smile and batting her dark eyes at him.

Stokes relaxed his stiffened posture as he walked over and shook her hand. "The Halloween Dance is one of the best events of the whole year. You should both come."

He spoke to both of them, but didn't take his eyes off of Gabby, or let go of her hand until she pulled it away and sat back down.

"It sounds like fun, but I'm afraid I'll be going back to New York before the weekend."

"Gabby is interviewing the police commissioner of New York City coming up for an article she's writing."

"You're a writer, too? New York City sure is full of attractive writers," Stokes observed.

"And, deputies can be full of shit, too," a deep voice announced from the hallway door. Ben stood in the doorway in his full brown police uniform.

Stokes shot right up almost at attention as Ben walked in.

"Did you take care of that traffic situation at the school?" he asked Stokes.

"Yes, sir. All the buses are in and out and the kids are safe inside."

Ben didn't say anything, but just stared at the deputy.

"I better go check and see if I have any messages. It was nice meeting you, Gabby. Jaime, it's good to know you're out of the hospital." He didn't wait to hear their replies, but quickly left the room through the door that Ben had just come out from.

"You shouldn't scare him like that," Jaime insisted.

"I didn't scare him. I embarrassed him by catching him ogling Gabby."

"What, he's not allowed to flirt while on duty?" Gabby asked.

"No, he's supposed to be interested in the waitress at the corner restaurant. Why don't you ladies come into my office and I'll update you on Jaime's case."

Jaime and Gabby followed Ben into his office and took the seats in front of his desk. Ben walked to the file cabinet where the coffee pot sat on top. "Coffee?" he turned and asked.

Both ladies held up their travel mugs showing him they already had some. "Mine's decaf," Jaime pointed out.

He poured himself a cup and then sat down behind his desk, taking a drink before sitting down his cup.

"Is there anything new on my case?" Jaime asked.

"The State Police picked up your camera this morning and will check it for prints."

"I don't suppose they will come up with something as quickly as they do on television, will they?"

"No, not that fast. But, as a favor to me, they are going to put a rush on it."

"Are you going to be questioning anyone?" Gabby asked.

"Like who?" Ben took another drink of his coffee.

"You need to question Clayton Spencer and Malcolm Cook, especially Malcolm Cook. They found those Indian bones after the Murdock's disappeared. And, I just know Malcolm is the one who pushed me over the cliff."

"I'm not going to question Clayton Spencer."

"Why not?" Jaime interrupted.

"Because I'm not investigating the Murdock family disappearance. I'm only looking into your accident."

"But, they're related."

"We don't know that yet. Now, I'll talk to Malcolm, but in my own way and my own time. In the meantime, I want you to stay away from him; both of you." His stare went from Jaime to Gabby and then back to Jaime again.

Gabby didn't say a word, just sipped her coffee.

"Fine," Jaime snapped. "We have other things to do."

"And, what would that be?" Ben asked.

"We're going back to the newspaper office and print those articles again. In one of them, it mentions the name of the professor at Indiana University that determined that those bones belonged to Indians. Gabby and I are then going to drive up to the university and talk to him."

"Why don't you just call him?" Ben asked. "It's about a two-hour drive to get there."

"I can be more persuasive in person."

"She can," Gabby agreed, nodding her head.

"Don't I know it," Ben added.

Ben quickly stood up as the ladies tried to leave. "What's the rush to get up there today?"

"Gabby will be leaving in a few days and the doctor hasn't cleared me to drive yet, unless you want to take me."

"I told you, it's..."

"...not an official investigation yet." Jaime finished his sentence.

"Are you sure you're up for the trip?"

"I feel great today."

"Well, just don't over do it."

"Don't worry. I won't let her," Gabby promised, as they walked out of his office.

"Let me know what you find out," he called after them.

They stopped next to Angie's desk and turned around. By this time, Ben was standing at his door. "Why? You aren't officially investigating it," Jaime jeered.

Angie, Deputy Stokes, and a jail trustee all looked at Ben for his reply. "I'm just curious, that's all." He turned back to his office and closed the door before someone else could get the last word in.

The ladies waited for Angie to push the button to let them out the door. It's buzzed and Jaime turned the knob and stepped out into the lobby.

Before going out the door, Gabby stopped and turned around. "Bye, Deputy." She winked.

Back in their car, Jaime gave Gabby directions to the newspaper office that was one turn and two blocks away. They parked on the street in front of the office and went in.

Inside, they found the lobby empty, but the bell on the door soon brought Sam Morgan to the front.

"Good morning, Mr. Morgan. It looks like you're a little short-handed today," Jaime observed.

"She's on a break."

"Is your brother here?"

"No, he had to drive over to Whitley today."

"That's okay. This is an associate of mine from New York, Gabrielle Santoro."

Morgan just stared at her.

"Pleasure to meet your, Mr. Morgan." Gabby shook his hand.

"We need to use your archives again, if you don't mind?" Jaime asked.

He let out a deep breath. "I suppose. Aren't you finished with that article yet?"

"Not quite, but things are really starting to come together. Thanks, I remember the way." Jaime started down the hallway with Gabby following. She opened the door to the basement, turned on the light and they started down the steps. Morgan slammed the door behind them and they jumped at the echoing sound.

"You weren't kidding about this feeling like a dungeon," Gabby commented, following her to the microfilm reader.

"Good, no one put the reels away yet." Jaime sat down and threaded the film through the machine and began scrolling through the copies of newspaper pages until she stopped at one. "Here it is."

Gabby pulled a chair up next to Jaime and took paper and pen out.

"Dr. Norman Cabot, Director of the Indiana University Department of Archeology." Jaime read out loud and Gabby wrote it down. "There's no quotes from him in the article, but it says he's the one who examined the bones and determined they were Native American."

"So, I guess we're off to..." Gabby stared at the screen. "Bloomington, Indiana."

"Yes, we are. But, first, I want to stop by the Public Library to make some copies and get directions off the computer."

Jaime printed off the other articles again that had been stolen and then put everything away. When they walked back into the lobby, the receptionist had returned from her break and sat at the desk.

"Elaine, I printed five pages today. Can you put those on the bill for my magazine to pay?"

"Sure, you just need to sign for them."

"Sign? I didn't have to do that before."

"Something new that Mr. Morgan started," the receptionist explained, handing Jaime a form to sign.

"Which Mr. Morgan?" Jaime asked, as she signed.

"Sam," Elaine replied in a low voice.

"Sam?"

"Yes, but don't tell anyone I told you." She turned to look down the hallway.

"I won't say a word. Thanks." She handed the signed form back to the receptionist.

The ladies left and headed to the library. "I want to make a copy of these pages for you and Ben to keep in case something happens again. Turn right at the next block and the library is a few blocks down on the left."

"Why didn't you print extra copies of the articles at the newspaper office?" Gabby asked.

"I didn't want anyone there knowing that I have more than one copy."

Gabby parked the car on the street next the library and went inside. Jaime heard the familiar creek of the door as she pushed it open.

Annie stood in her usual spot behind the main counter. "Jaime, it's so good to see you again. I heard about your fall. How are you?'

"I'm feeling much better now. How did you hear about it?"

"Why it's on the front page of this week's paper. It came out today. You didn't know?"

"No. I had no idea."

"Who's your friend?" Annie nodded toward Gabby.

"I'm sorry. This is my friend, Gabrielle. She is from New York also."

"Gabby, this is Annie Sampson, the County Librarian."

Gabby stepped up to the counter and extended her hand to the gray-haired lady. "It's a pleasure to meet you."

Annie shook hands with her. "Are you here to write a story about our little town, too?"

"No, I came here when Jaime got hurt. I'll actually be heading back to the city this week."

"Annie, I need to use the copy machine and a computer."

"They're both around the corner, honey," she replied, pointing toward the corner by the desk. "It's ten cents per copy."

"I remember." They stepped around to the copy machine first and Jaime started making copies of the articles. When the last copy shot out of the machine, Jaime counted them and then handed a set to Gabby. "If something happens to my copies, I may have to call you to email me your set, if Ben is too busy to get me his copy."

"I'll scan them as soon as I get back to the office," Gabby promised.

The rest of the copies went into Jaime's backpack.

Next, she moved to the computer and quickly printed out directions to the Archeology building on the Indiana University campus. They came back around the corner to the front counter where Annie, now seated, still worked on some books. Jaime stepped up to the counter and handed Annie two one-dollar bills. "All together, I copied and printed eighteen copies."

Annie retrieved two dimes from the drawer and then put the dollars inside. "Let me write your receipt."

"There's no need for that." Jaime took the dimes and dropped them into a small pocket on the side of her pack.

"It's really more for me than you. The County makes me account for every cent here." Annie tore the receipt out of the small book and handed it to her.

"Thanks. Do you know how Eleanor Cook is doing?" Jaime asked.

"Well, you know she's in a nursing home?"

"Yes, I heard."

"I understand Malcolm is telling folks she's in a coma," Annie expressed in a low voice.

Jaime leaned in closer. "Isn't she?"

"Well, Josephine, who works in the laundry at the nursing where Eleanor is at, told me the other day that she's awake, but not saying much."

"Is that right? What nursing home is she in?"

Annie took a step back and looked to her right and then to her left, stepped back to the counter and whispered, "She's in the Whitley Manor. It's one of those fancy smancy private places. She has her own room and a personal staff. It costs an arm and leg to stay there. Not many people around here can afford it."

"I wonder who is paying then."

"Oh, Eleanor's got plenty of money. Her late husband found a coal mine back on their property years before he died and blasted all the ore out and sold it for a fortune."

"Well, it's wonderful that Eleanor has such good care." Jaime turned to Gabby. "I think we should be going now. We have lots of work to do today."

"Could you please not tell anyone about Eleanor? I wouldn't want to get Josephine into any trouble," Annie asked.

"Of course, I won't say a thing. Oh, I almost forgot. Here is that County History book that you let me read. It was so interesting. Thank you."

"You're welcome." Jaime and Gabby started for the door, but Annie called after them, "You tell that good-looking sheriff that I said hi."

"I will. Thanks again."

Once back in the car, Gabby started the engine and pulled out, following the directions to the university they had printed at the library.

"That was interesting news to learn about Mrs. Cook," Gabby mentioned.

"Yes. I think I'll go pay her a visit this week. I want to see what she has to say about the day of her fall."

"You're going to have to go solo on that visit. While you were talking to the librarian, I was on the computer booking my flight home for tomorrow."

"I wish you didn't have to leave so soon. I could really use your help here."

"Sweetie, I think you have everything under control, including Sheriff Ben."

"Like I said before, long distance relationships don't work. Take a right at that stoplight and follow the highway north," Jaime related, looking at the directions.

"All I'm saying is that it would be a shame if he were Mr. Right and you didn't take a chance." The light changed to green and Gabby followed the traffic ahead of her, until she could turn.

Jaime didn't reply, but instead looked out the window at the beautiful red, orange, and yellow trees as they drove farther north.

* * * *

Two hours later, they reached Bloomington, Indiana and followed the signs and their directions to the university. They parked at a parking garage and started on their four-block walk to the Archaeology Department.

Students filled the sidewalks on both sides of the street, all with packs on their backs and either a cell phone or an IPod in their ears.

"I've never so many big limestone buildings." Gabby noticed all around them.

"I read that Indiana is known for its limestone. This sure brings back memories."

"You went to school in Pennsylvania, right?"

"Yes. The campus was a lot like this one. What was your campus like?" Jaime asked, just as a student sped by on a bicycle nearly knocking her over.

"I went to culinary school, remember? It was in one big building, but once I got to New York, I took journalism classes at Columbia. I actually only need a few more classes to earn my degree."

"You should finish and get that degree."

"I know, but I'm doing what I want and really don't need a degree for that."

"Here's the Archeology building."

They climbed the fifteen steps up to the glass doors and entered the building. A female student stood behind the Information counter. "Can I help you?"

"Yes, do you have a Dr. Norman Cabot on staff here?" Jaime asked.

The student ran her finger down a list of names on the wall. "No ma'am. There's no one on staff by that name."

"I know he used to teach here. Would someone have his current address?"

"Let me call someone who might be able to help you. You can wait over there." the student pointing to a couch in the lobby.

Jaime and Gabby took a seat on the couch and several minutes later, an older woman with salt and pepper-colored hair wearing gold-rimmed glasses approached them.

"I'm Dr. Francis Johnson, Director of Research here at the school. Can I be of some help?"

The ladies stood and Jaime extended her hand to the doctor. "I'm Jaime Wilson and this is Gabrielle Santoro. We're from *Real Mystery Magazine* and we're trying to locate a former professor for an interview." Jaime immediately noticed the feel of roughness of Dr. Johnson's hand. No doubt from years of excavating sites. Her leathery looking skin marked evidence of frequent sun exposure.

"If you'll follow me to my office, I'll see if I can help you." Dr. Johnson led them through the door next to the Information Desk and down a long hallway to her office. The doctor took a seat behind her desk with Jaime and Gabby sitting in the chairs in front.

"What's the name of the professor you're looking for?"

"Dr. Norman Cabot," Jaime replied.

"That name doesn't sound familiar," Dr. Johnson commented, as she typed on the keyboard.

"How long have you been here at the university?" Gabby asked.

"Almost ten years." The professor continued to type.

"When would Dr. Cabot have taught here?"

"About thirty years ago."

The doctor typed more. "I'm sorry. I don't find anyone by that name."

"Are you sure?" Gabby asked.

"I'm positive. We keep a list of all past and present professors for guest lecturers and there is no one with that name listed. What made you think he taught here?"

Jaime took out a copy of the newspaper article and handed it to Dr. Johnson, who studied it for a few moments. She then laid the article down and typed some more on the computer. "I don't know what the police were talking about in that article, but there were no skeletal bones logged into our system around that date thirty years ago." She handed the article back to Jaime. "Could it have possibly been another university?"

"I don't know. That article said it was here."

"Let me give you some contact names and phone numbers at some other schools in Indiana that have archaeology departments." A few seconds later, the printer shot out a sheet of paper that Dr. Johnson handed to Jaime. "Try these and maybe they might be able to help."

"Thank you."

"Can I ask why you are interested in those skeletons?" the doctor asked.

"I'm working on an article about a missing family and these bones were found in the general area of the disappearance several years afterward."

"And, you think these are their bones?"

Jaime thought for a second about her answer. "I'm hoping Dr. Cabot might remember these bones and give me a quote for my article."

"I see. Well, good luck with your search for him."

Jaime and Gabby shook hands with Dr. Johnson and left. Back at the car, Jaime checked her watch.

"It's almost four o'clock and I'm starved. Let's find someplace to eat before we leave town."

"I'm all for that," Gabby agreed. After paying at the parking garage, she pulled the car out into traffic.

The stream of cars led them downtown, where they saw a sports bar and restaurant sign and decided to eat there. During their meal, Jaime's cell phone rang.

"It's Ben," she said, looking at the Caller ID. "Hello."

"Where are you? I thought you'd be back by now."

"We're still in Bloomington. As soon as we finish our dinner, we'll be on our way home."

"Okay. Did you find the professor?"

"Not exactly. I'll tell you about it when we get back."

"Call me, if you have problems."

"I will. Bye." Jaime closed her phone and put it back in her purse. She signaled to the waitress for the bill.

"What did he want?" Gabby asked.

"He was worried about us."

"Do you realize what you said to him?"

Jaime thought for a second. "I told him we'd be heading back soon."

Gabby chuckled. "No, you told him you'd be on the way *home* soon."

"No! I didn't say home, did I?"

"Yes, you did."

"Why would I say that?"

"Whether you like it or not, I think you're getting cozy to the idea of you and Sheriff Ben being together."

The waitress brought their check and Jaime handed an American Express card to her. "This one goes on my expense account," she told Gabby, as the waitress took the card and left.

"Admit it. You have fallen for Sheriff Ben."

Jaime hesitated before answering. "I do have feelings for him, but it's got to be an infatuation. I can't fall for someone that fast. We don't even know each other that well."

"You slept with him, right?"

"Now, you're going to call me a slut, too?" Jaime joked.

"No, but if you slept together, you know each other well enough."

"That's ridiculous. You don't understand what I mean."

"Yes, I do understand. I also know that you haven't had a date in months and now you have found someone who truly cares for you."

"It won't work. I've tried a long-distance relationship once and it didn't work."

"Right. You were in college and still a teenager. Of course it didn't work. You're making excuses. You're afraid."

"Maybe you're right. Maybe I am afraid. But, my career is going so well, a relationship at this point could really screw things up."

The waitress returned with the credit card and receipt to sign. As soon as Jaime signed it, the ladies gathered their purses and walked out of the bar.

Gabby continued the previous conversation out on the sidewalk. "You know, sometimes there are things more important than a career."

"I know," Jaime replied, nonchalantly, as she window-shopped at the stores along the street. As far as she was concerned, the subject was over. "Oh, look a T-shirt store with college shirts. Let's go in. We both need to some souvenirs from our trip to Indiana."

"Okay, but I think your souvenir is sitting back at his house, with his dog, and waiting for you to come *home*."

"Stop that," Jaime reacted, only half serious about making Gabby actually stop. She pushed open the door and went inside the store.

Two and a half hours later, the ladies walked into Ben's house and found him sitting on the couch with his feet up, dog on the floor next to him, eating popcorn and watching television.

"I was beginning to worry about you." He turned the sound down with the remote.

"You don't look like you're worried," Jaime noted.

"In fact, you look rather relaxed," Gabby added, plopping down in the chair, leaving only the couch next to Ben for Jaime to sit. She sat her bags down before sitting on the far end of the couch.

"Oh my god, I should have known. You two went shopping, didn't you?" He laughed.

"We went to one store and bought some souvenirs of Indiana," Jaime stated.

"It's true. That's what we did," Gabby added. "T-shirts, notepads, key chains and a coffee mug; want to see them?"

"No, I live here. I've seen it all before." He still chuckled and took a drink from a bottle of beer. He moved the bowl of popcorn over so Jaime could reach it. "So, what did you find out?"

Jaime and Gabby took turns telling him about not finding the professor, or a log of the skeletons being brought to the university, all while munching the popcorn and drinking beer that Gabby had brought from the kitchen.

"I'm going to start calling the other universities tomorrow and see what I can find out."

"While you ladies were having fun in college town, I turned up something interesting." Ben handed Jaime an old worn file folder.

She looked through the pages inside. "This is the missing file on the Murdock family disappearance from your department."

"Yes, it is."

"Where did you get it?"

"Clayton Spencer had it."

"Who is Clayton Spencer?" Gabby asked.

"He's a former sheriff here," Ben answered. "He even added an extra page of notes in the back of the file."

Jaime quickly turned to the extra page. "I still don't trust him. Why did he have it?"

"He said it has always been a pet project for him because no one ever solved it. Which is true. If you remember, you first met him when he was giving a talk at the local Historical Society meeting."

"What did you say to him about having the file?" Jaime asked.

"I made sure he understood the repercussions that could have occurred from him having it."

"*Could* occur?" What he did was theft. He should have charges filed against him."

"That's not going to happen. Clayton Spencer spent forty years in law enforcement in the county. He took the file because this was the one case he was sorry that never got solved. He hoped all through the years that something would turn up on the case."

"And, you believe him?" Jaime asked.

"Yes, I do. Well, I believe some of it."

"I hate to break up this party because we're having so much fun.

But, I am flying back to New York tomorrow and need to pack and then get some sleep. I do have one problem though. Jaime isn't supposed to drive yet and I need a ride to the airport. Are there any taxies or buses around here I can take?"

"I can drive," Jaime boosted. "I've felt great today."

"No, you're not driving until the doctor says it's okay," Ben instructed. "There's no buses or taxies, but I can take you, if you don't mind going in my truck."

"That would be great. Thank you."

"What's wrong with taking my rental car? We'd be more comfortable."

"I'm not listed on your rental contract," he reminded her.

"Neither is Gabby, but she drove it."

"Actually, I am on it. When I arrived at the airport after your fall, I was able to get added on to it by showing my credentials with the magazine."

"Especially after I told them why she was here," Ben added.

"You should have seen him. He was very persuasive in his uniform," Gabby teased. "My flight leaves at eleven in the morning."

"It's a long drive, so we should leave around nine o'clock," Ben suggested.

"With that settled, I'm heading to pack and then sleep. See you both in the morning."

"Goodnight," Ben called, as Gabby left the room. He turned to Jaime. "How much longer will you be here?"

"My deadline is a few weeks away, but I may ask for an extension."

"Oh."

"You know, after Gabby leaves, I should move back to that inn and get out of your hair," Jaime suggested, getting off of the couch and moving toward her room.

"No." Ben jumped up, nearly tripping over the dog and placed himself between her and the door. "I don't want you to move out."

Jaime didn't know what to say, but Ben did.

"For your safety, of course. We still don't know who pushed you off the cliff and I don't think anyone will try anything while you're here."

"I'm sure I'd be okay at the inn. It seemed pretty secure to me." She turned, but Ben caught her arm.

"That's not the only reason I want you to stay."

She told herself to pull away from him, but she couldn't. It became a tug-of-war between her heart and her head, with her heart winning.

She turned back toward him.

"I have feelings for you, Jaime. And, I think you feel the same way."

This time she stepped out of his hold. "You know this won't work between us. I live and work in New York and Royal is your home. Relationships are hard enough without there being eight-hundred miles between us."

"It wouldn't have to be for long. I only have two years left on my term as sheriff. After that, I could move to New York and find work there."

"I won't let you do that."

"You work from here then. Can't writers work from home and email in their stories?"

"I don't want to talk about this anymore. I should go see if Gabby needs any help." She quickly walked to the door to Gabby's room, knocked, and went right in.

Inside the room, she found Gabby standing by the bed not really doing anything, but looking very guilty.

"You were listening to us, weren't you?" Jaime asked.

"Not at first, but I couldn't help hearing since you were both outside my door."

"So, what do you think?" she asked, sitting on the bed.

"I think you're crazy for not accepting his offer of a relationship and he's right, you could just as easily work at your job from here." Gabby sat down next to Jaime.

"Not if I become the Assistant Editor."

"Well yeah, there's that."

Jaime jumped up off the bed. "What am I thinking? I shouldn't even be considering this. Are you packed yet?" she asked, changing the subject.

"Not completely. I noticed you didn't say anything to Ben about finding out about Eleanor Cook being awake."

"I want to go visit her first and see for myself before dragging Ben along."

"Just be careful while checking into some of this stuff," Gabby warned. "I wish I didn't have to leave." She got up and went over to hug Jaime.

"Me, too." She let out a deep breath. "I probably should get to bed. We both need our sleep."

"Goodnight, sweetie."

"See you in the morning." Jaime opened the bedroom door and

found the living room dark. In the light coming from Gabby's room, she could see Ben sleeping on the couch. Gently closing the door behind her, she tiptoed to her room.

# Chapter Ten

"I really wish you didn't have to leave so soon," Jaime told Gabby while standing at the airport security gate. Ben stood nearby as the ladies said their goodbyes.

"I wish I could stay longer too, but I can't risk losing that interview I have scheduled."

"I understand." Jaime gave her a hug.

"Have fun with the sheriff," Gabby whispered into Jaime's ear. "Make sure you try out his handcuffs."

Jaime stepped back and gave Gabby a wide-eyed look, knowing Ben stood close and might have heard. She could feel her face getting warm.

"Ben." Gabby turned to the sheriff. "It was a pleasure meeting you." She gave him a hug and then stepped back. "Watch over Jaime and don't let anything happen to her."

"I'll take good care of her. It was nice meeting you, too. Have a good flight."

Gabby waved one last time to both of them as she went through security and onto her gate. Jaime and Ben headed to the parking garage and the long drive back to Royal.

Once on the road, Jaime worried that Ben would bring up their relationship again, a topic she wanted to avoid. Riding in the truck, she almost felt like a captive prisoner with no place to escape.

Ben finally broke the silence. "It will still be fairly early in the afternoon when we get home. I'll have to go to work for the rest of the day."

"Okay."

"I guess you'll just stay home?"

"Yes. I'll work on my article and catch up on some e-mails while at your house." Jaime wanted to make sure she said house and not home after Gabby had pointed out how she had misspoken the night before.

"I should be home in time for dinner. I haven't bought any groceries for a while, would you like to go out for dinner tonight?" he asked.

*A date? Is he asking me out on a date?* "I suppose that would be okay, but don't you think you need to get some food in the house instead?"

"You're probably right, especially since you'll be there during the day. We could drive over to Whitley get a quick bite to eat and then stop by the supermarket for groceries."

"That sounds like a plan."

"Would you mind making a grocery list this afternoon?" he asked.

"Sure, I can do that, but I'm not sure what kind of food you like."

"I eat just about anything and I'll be with you at the store, so don't worry about that."

"I bet you live on sandwiches and microwave meals."

"Nope. I'm a pretty good cook, but I do keep some frozen dinners on hand for the nights I work too late to cook."

"That's good to know."

"When do you go back to the doctor?" he asked.

"Tomorrow. Hopefully, he'll clear me to drive again. You live too far away from town for me to be able to walk where I need to go. In New York, I could walk or take the subway when I needed to meet someone. I'm going to need to interview some more people here to finish my article."

"I don't think you need to be interviewing anyone unless I'm with you."

"No, that won't work. They might not talk openly if you're hovering by me." She had already planned on slipping off later today to go visit Eleanor Cook at the Convalescent Center in Whitley and no way did she want him coming with her for that visit.

An hour later, Ben pulled the truck into his driveway. Once inside, he went to his bedroom to change into his uniform and Jaime to the kitchen to make a pitcher of tea. After the tea started brewing in the machine, she took a seat at the table to start on the grocery list.

Always being a sucker for a man in uniform, she couldn't help noticing how sexy he looked when he walked into the kitchen.

"Is the tea ready yet?"

"What?" She was forced to snap back to reality from the rather erotic daydream that spun through her head about getting Ben out of that uniform.

"Never mind." He took a two tall glasses from the cabinet and poured himself a glass of the freshly brewed tea and took a long drink.

"Aren't you going to sweeten that?"

After emptying the whole glass, he answered, "No. I don't usually sweeten my tea or coffee." He took the second glass of tea to Jaime and sat it on the table. She put two spoons of sugar in and stirred.

"I guess I'll mark sugar off the list," she joked.

"I need to get going," he said, turning to leave the kitchen.

Jaime followed him into the living room.

"Do you know how to use a handgun?" he asked.

"Yes. Why?"

He walked over to the desk in the corner near the door and opened the drawer. Taking out a pistol, he slid out the magazine and handed both to her. "Show me."

She took the gun and first pulled the slide back to check for a round in the chamber. Taking the magazine from him, she smacked it against her thigh and then inserted it into the handle of the gun. Pulling back on the slide, she cycled a round into the gun's chamber and then put the safety on before handing it back to him, butt first.

"Where did you learn that?" he asked.

"From an old boyfriend. We used to go to the gun range and shoot all the time."

Ben put the gun back in the desk and then sat on the couch. "Sit next to me."

Jaime did as he suggested.

"Put your hand under the coffee table and tell me what you feel."

She reached under the table and felt what he was talking about. "It's a smaller gun taped underneath."

"Right. It's a .32 caliber with six rounds in the magazine and one in the chamber. The safety is on. There's another one in the drawer by my bed and a shotgun in the closet. All of them are loaded."

"Why are you telling me this?"

"I don't want to scare you, but I want you to be prepared since you'll be here alone." The dog barked at Ben. "Okay, okay, you'll be here to protect her, too," he said to the dog.

"I'll be fine. I'm going to move my stuff back into the other bedroom today. You need your room back."

Ben rose. "I've got to go. Keep the doors and windows locked and don't let anyone in. If you need me, call my cell phone first. If I don't answer, call my office. They can get a hold of me by radio." He looked down at the dog sitting at Jaime's feet. "Watch over her, Jake."

Jaime stood at the door and watched Ben drive off to work in his patrol car. The dog began whining and scratched at the screen door.

"I bet you need to take a walk after being inside all morning." She opened the door and watched to make sure he didn't run off. After taking care of his business by the Maple tree, Jake trotted back to the porch and walked in through the door that she held open for him, and closed it making sure it locked behind her.

Jaime looked at her watch. She had wanted to visit Eleanor today, but now was afraid she wouldn't make it back before Ben got back home. She looked down at the dog. "Well Jake, I think I'll fix myself something to eat. Doesn't that sound like an exciting way to spend the day?"

"Woof," the dog replied.

In the kitchen, she took a Turkey Pot Pie out of the freezer and popped it in the microwave to cook. She sat up her laptop on the kitchen table to work on the article.

"It won't be long until I'm all finished here and back in New York," she told the dog. "I'm sure going to miss you Jake, and your master, too."

The dog walked over from his rug and put his head on her lap for petting. She obliged him.

"You know what? You deserve a reward for being such a good guard dog. I think I saw a bag of dog treats in here the other day." Looking through the cabinets and drawers, she finally found the bag. "Here you go." She handed the dog a chewy morsel from the bag.

"What's this?" From the same drawer, she pulled out a five-by-seven framed picture of Ben and a woman. Jaime recognized the cityscape in the background as Chicago. The photo had been taken of the couple at the top of the Sears Tower.

"This must be Leann, his girlfriend who died. She's beautiful and they look so happy."

Jaime looked at the photo and wondered if she could make him as happy if she agreed to a relationship. The microwave beeped signaling that her food was done. She put the photo and the dog treats back in the drawer. "I don't feel much like writing this afternoon after all. My head's starting to hurt a little, so I think I'll watch some television instead."

"Woof."

She knew that bark meant that Jake agreed with her. Closing the lid on top of her laptop, she poured herself a second glass of tea and took it and her food into the living room.

The next thing she knew, Ben was waking her up from a deep sleep.

"Jaime, Jaime, wake up."

"Woof."

"Quiet, Jake."

"I'm awake." Jaime sat up on the couch and yawned. "How long have I been asleep?"

"The ice in your tea has melted and your food looks barely touched. I'd say you've been out for a while."

"What time is it?" she asked, trying to focus on the clock sitting on the fireplace mantel.

"It's five-thirty. I had to process two prisoners and couldn't get away on time.,

"That's okay. Since I fell asleep, I haven't gotten ready yet." She ran her hand through her hair, knowing it had to be a mess.

"You needed your rest. You've been going non-stop since you got out of the hospital."

"I suppose you're right. Let me change my clothes and run a comb through my hair and we can be on our way to the supermarket."

"There might be a change in the plan. It's raining and I hate to get groceries in the rain. I thought we'd put it off until tomorrow and just go out for dinner."

"That sounds fine. Since I didn't eat my lunch, I'm starved. Let me get changed."

At the same time, they both started walking toward Ben's bedroom and then stopped.

"I'm so sorry. I didn't get my things moved back to the guest room yet."

"There's plenty of time for that."

They entered the bedroom and Jaime quickly picked out some clothes to wear and grabbed her makeup bag. "I'll be as quick as I can," she called, rushing out the door to the bathroom down the hall, leaving him to change in his own room.

As Jaime washed her face and applied a little makeup, she couldn't help feeling a little nervous about their *date*. She put on olive green slacks and a black sweater and checked herself in the full-length mirror. She smoothed everything down, took a deep breath, and walked to the living room where she found Ben waiting.

He looked so ruggedly handsome in dress jeans, navy blue button down shirt, and hiking boots. Her heart did a little flutter at the sight of him. *Wow*, she thought to herself. "Did I take too long?" she asked.

Ben smiled. "It was worth the wait. You look beautiful."

"Thank you. You look pretty good yourself."

They both grabbed a jacket and headed out to Ben's truck.

When they reached Whitley, about a forty-five minute drive, Jaime immediately noticed that located on the edge of town was the Whitley Manor Convalescent Center where Eleanor Cook now lived. *At least it will be easy for me to find it tomorrow.*

She and Ben arrived at a German restaurant and went inside. They were seated in the back of a large room with murals of German drawings on the walls. A short time later, the waitress came and took their food and drink orders, leaving them to their conversation.

"I'm going to call the other universities tomorrow and see if I can track down Dr. Cabot."

"Have you tried an Internet search for him?"

"That's the first place I looked, but didn't find anything."

"Isn't that a little unusual?" Ben asked.

"Actually, it is. I would have thought with a PhD in Archeology, some of his published papers would have been online."

At that moment, the waitress brought their drinks and right behind her was Kenneth Morgan and his wife.

"Hello, Sheriff. I didn't think you ever left the county."

Ben stood to greet them. "I occasionally find time to get away. Kenneth, you've met Jaime Wilson?" Ben nodded his head toward Jaime and sat back down.

"Yes, we've become acquainted from her many trips to the newspaper office. This is my wife, Helen." He looked to Jaime.

"It's nice to see you again, Mrs. Morgan." Jaime looked over at Ben. "I met Mrs. Morgan at the market in town a few weeks ago."

"Jaime, you must call me, Helen."

"Thank you, Helen."

"Tell me, dear, how much longer are you going to be staying in our lovely town?"

Jaime looked to Ben for help, but all he did was look back and smile. "I'm not really sure, maybe a couple more weeks."

"Wonderful! I am sure we'll be seeing each other around town. Oh, I just had a splendid thought. Would you be willing to come to a meeting of the Women of Royal? You could speak to us about what it's like to be a big city writer," Helen suggested.

She had put Jaime on the spot. "I...ah...I suppose...I..."

"Fantastic. I'll have to check the calendar when I get home and let you know the date. I can get in touch with you at Ben's, right?"

"Helen," her husband chided.

"Let me give you my card." Jaime pulled one of her business cards out of her purse and handed it to Helen. "This has my cell phone number on it. That's the best way to reach me."

"I think we had better go," Mr. Morgan stated.

"It was nice seeing you, Kenneth, Helen," Ben stood as they walked away.

"You do realize we'll be the main topic of conversation of the town gossip's next breakfast?" Jaime pointed out.

"I do and I don't care anymore."

Their food finally arrived and they dug in. Ben immediately started carving his steak and Jaime couldn't decide what to try first on her seafood platter.

"Do you still think Kenneth Morgan is involved in the Murdock family's disappearance?" Ben asked.

"At the time, it was a feeling I had. Now, I'm thinking his brother Sam may be involved instead."

"Why do you think he's involved?"

She swallowed the bite of food she had just taken. "Every time I'm at the newspaper office, Sam watches me. It's creepy."

Ben laughed. "Sam has never been accused of being overly social. He's been a loner for as long as I can remember, except for that time he was married."

"Sam? Who would marry him?"

Ben took a drink of his beer. "He was married to Malcolm Cook's sister, Louise. Best I can remember she died at a young age."

"That's terrible."

"Yeah, from what I've heard people say, he and Malcolm were best friends; still are, I reckon."

"Really? Best friends, that's very interesting." She made a mental note to check on that later.

"Do I see those investigative wheels turning in that pretty head of yours?"

"No, but its information that's good to know."

After they finished their meal, they left the restaurant and headed back to Royal. At a stoplight, a car with a couple teenagers pulled up next to them. Jaime noticed they were wearing Halloween masks.

"Isn't it illegal to wear a mask and drive?" she asked.

"Not so much illegal as it is dangerous and stupid, but what do you expect from teenagers? Halloween is next week and there'll be lots of mischief for me to deal with."

After crossing back into Butler County, Ben took a turn off of the highway.

"Where are we going?" Jaime asked.

"I want to show you a place where another mystery has gone unsolved."

"Another one? How many do you have in this county?" she asked.

Ben turned onto a single gravel lane and followed the winding road. Without any moonlight, Jaime couldn't see anything except what the headlights lit ahead of them.

Finally, Ben stopped the truck and turned off the lights and engine. The cab of the truck became even darker, except for the light from his police radio until he turned it off, too.

"Where are we?" she asked.

"Look around and see."

Once her eyes adjusted to the darkness, she could make out the shapes of tombstones outside of the truck.

"We're at a cemetery?"

"A haunted cemetery."

"I don't believe in ghosts." Jaime shivered.

"You're cold. Why don't you move over next to me," he suggested.

She scooted across the seat next to him and he put his arm around her rubbing her arm to warm her.

"Many, many years ago, a young couple came to this cemetery late one night to look for a ghost. They disappeared. Never to be seen again."

"Really? Tell me about this ghost." She snuggled a little closer to him.

"The ghost is a young woman who was killed in a hit and run accident. The legend goes that she is looking for the person who killed her. Many people see her walking around here at night."

As he spoke, he slowly leaned toward her until their lips touched.

"What...happened...to...the...couple?" she asked between kisses.

"No one ever saw them again."

The next thing Jaime knew they had slid down flat on the seat of the truck as she and Ben continued kissing.

She felt his hand move under her sweater, making his way to her bra. Her hands were just as busy trying to get to his belt when his cell phone started ringing.

"Damn. I have to answer this." They both moved back to a sitting position with Jaime still next to him.

"Hello...What? When did it start...Okay, I'm on the way" He hung up the call. "The newspaper office in Royal is on fire. We have to go." He turned his police radio back on and they left the cemetery.

As they listened to the traffic on the radio about the fire, Jaime asked. "How bad is it?"

"Stokes said the building was fully engulfed by the time the fire department got there."

A few minutes down the road, they topped a hill and could see a yellow glow rising up from the horizon. The closer they got to town, the larger the glow became.

With all the cars and trucks from the volunteer firefighters, on-lookers, and fire trucks, Ben had to park several blocks away.

He quickly got out, but Jaime stopped him.

"Wait." She ran to his side of the truck where he stood. "Wipe the lipstick off of your face."

With the sleeve of his shirt, he wiped across his face. "How's that?"

She took a good look at his face. "That's better. Now, go."

Ben took off in a trot through the crowd. Jaime followed at a lesser pace. When she caught up with him, he stood between Deputy Stokes and Kenneth Morgan. Morgan's brother, Sam stood next to them. In the crowd, she saw Mrs. Morgan, tears running down her cheeks as she watched her husband's business go up in flames. Several other ladies comforted her.

"What time was the fire called in?" Ben asked.

"Dispatch got the call at nine-fifteen," Stokes replied. "The fire department arrived by nine-thirty."

"It's been burning this hot for thirty minutes? What kind of combustibles have you got in there that would fuel the fire so much?" Ben asked Morgan.

"We're a newspaper office and while we contract out the printing of the newspaper, we still print many other things. We have paper and chemicals in there. Although, the chemicals are supposed to be locked up in a metal cabinet at the end of each day."

"Who would have been the last person to leave tonight?" Ben asked.

"I left at six to take my wife to dinner and Sam was still there."

"Sam, were you the last to leave tonight?" Stokes asked.

"I was."

"And everything was fine when you left?" Ben jumped back in.

"Yes."

Jaime didn't think Sam Morgan sounded very forthcoming with his short answers to Ben's questions.

"What time did you leave?" Stokes asked.

"I left at six-thirty and went straight home. I suppose you're going to blame me for this," Sam Morgan snorted.

"Not at all, Sam. We're just trying to narrow down the timeline."

*Ben might not suspect him, but I do*, Jaime thought. She watched as the firefighters switched their battle from saving the newspaper office to keeping the nearby buildings from burning, too.

It took another hour to finally get the fire under control, at which time the building had burned to the ground. Luckily, the other buildings were saved from the live embers floating in the air.

The fire chief walked over to Ben and the group. "I'm going to call the State Fire Marshall in the morning and have him check the remains of the building for the cause."

"You think it was set on purpose?" Kenneth asked.

"As fast as the building burned, it's a possibility," Chief Blake suggested.

Ben pulled Jaime away from the group. "I'm going to have to stay here for most of the night and watch over the building. I'll have Deputy Stokes take you back to my place."

"Why don't I drive your truck and the deputy can bring you home later? I hate to take him away from here," she suggested.

"You aren't supposed to drive yet," he reminded her. "Besides, I don't want you going into an empty house alone."

*He does take good care of me*, she thought.

"Stokes," he called to the deputy, who immediately came over to them.

"Yes, sir."

"I want you to take Miss Wilson to my house. Go inside with her and do a complete walk-through of the house and make sure no one is in there before you leave."

"Sure thing, boss," Stokes replied. He led Jaime to his patrol car and they drove to Ben's home. Not much was said on the drive to Ben's home. They listened to the traffic on the police radio about the fire and Jaime asked Stokes a little about how old the building was and wondered how Kenneth Morgan could get the next issue of the newspaper out on time.

Upon arriving, Deputy Stokes did as Ben ordered. "Do you have the key?" he asked Jaime.

She handed him the spare key that Ben had made for her. He

opened the door and stepped inside first. Jake, the dog, looked up from his spot by the couch and slowly got up and yawned, then followed the pair to each room.

They walked into Ben's room first and Jaime suddenly realized that her suitcase and clothes were all over Ben's bed. In her haste to get dressed earlier, she hadn't put anything away or moved back to the guestroom. She noticed Stokes eyeing the mess.

"I really felt bad about using Ben room while Gabby was here. He had to sleep on the couch the whole time."

"Uh-huh," Stokes replied as he checked the closet for anyone hiding in there.

Once it checked okay, he moved to the guestroom. The room was immaculate, as if no one had slept in there for months.

"Gabby always leaves a room like she's never been there," Jaime explained, knowing that sounded really stupid.

Stokes appeared to have ignored her comment and then looked in Ben's office, the bathroom, and the kitchen. The whole time, Jaime and the dog followed behind him.

"Everything looks fine up here," he assured her. "I'll just check the basement and be on my way. You wait up here."

A few minutes later, the deputy emerged from the stairwell. "Everything checks out fine. All the doors and windows are locked. You should be safe."

"Thank you, Mark. I really appreciate you doing this. Could I ask you to do one more thing?"

"Sure."

"Since Gabby left today, I need to move my things out of Ben's room and back to the other bedroom. Would you mind caring my suitcase in there for me? I'm not supposed to lift anything heavy yet."

"I'd be glad to."

They went into Ben's room and she quickly threw most of her clothes in the suitcase and closed it. Deputy Stokes then carried it to the other room.

"Just put it on the bed. I'm sure Ben will be glad to get his room back. That couch had to be uncomfortable."

"Lock the door behind me and call 911 if anyone bothers you," Stokes instructed, as he went out the door.

"Thank you." She closed and locked the door, and watched the deputy drive away.

Jaime took a seat on the couch and turned the news on the

television. Slowly, her thoughts drifted back to her and Ben in his truck at the cemetery. She dreamed about how they would have made love like two teenagers in his parent's car. To feel his strong arms around her, to feel safe, and for a short amount of time, forgetting someone may be trying to kill her. Jake brushed against her leg and the daydream popped out of her head.

She patted his head. "I think I'll fix myself a cup of Chamomile tea," she announced.

With Jake following, she walked into the kitchen. While fixing her tea, she noticed Jake whining next to the front door.

"You need to go out, eh?"

"Woof," the dog barked back as if answering her.

She stood and went to the door letting him outside to do his thing and then back in. She quickly locked the door and peered through the window looking around for any movement outside.

On the couch, with Jake at her feet, Jaime grabbed the remote control and started surfing the channels. She decided on an old movie to watch. Two hours later, when the movie ended, she stretched her arms over her head and yawned. The dog had sprawled out on the floor next to the couch, sleeping.

*Squeak...Bang!*

Jaime jumped and the dog immediately sprung to his feet barking at the door.

"Jake, quiet. I'm sure that was just the house settling as the night cools."

She went to the front window and pulled the curtain aside peeking out. The light by the door illuminated the whole porch and all the way out to the driveway. Everything seemed at peace.

"See, I told you it was nothing." She looked at the clock on the wall that showed one o'clock.

The dog looked up at her and yawned.

"That's a good idea. We better go to sleep."

After checking the lock on the door again, she went to her bedroom, moved the suitcase to the floor, and pulled the covers down on the bed. Jake sat at the doorway, tongue hanging out of the side of his mouth. Jaime changed in to her New York Giants nightshirt and got into bed.

She looked over at the door where Jake still stood looking back at her. "I can't go to sleep with you staring at me. C'mon." Jaime patted the bed and Jake hopped up and circled before curling up at the foot of the bed. She turned off the light and before long she had reached a deep sleep.

# Chapter Eleven

The next morning, Jaime purposely stayed in bed until she heard Ben leave for work. She didn't want to lie if he asked about her plans for the day.

Only one more day until her doctor's appointment and hopefully she'd be cleared to drive, but she couldn't wait until then. She crawled out of bed. *Ben would never let me drive to visit Eleanor today, but what he doesn't know, won't hurt him. I can be there and back before he gets home from work.*

After getting dressed, Jaime went to the kitchen and fixed a piece of toast and added a slice of cheese on it before eating. She grabbed a caffeine-free diet soda and out the door she went. Driving out of the driveway she thought, *it feels so good to be behind the wheel again.*

The drive to Whitley had her heading east and the bright morning sun beamed right into her eyes. Even with sunglasses and the visor down, she had to squint to see the road.

By the time she arrived at the Whitley Manor Convalescent Center, she had developed a headache. *Maybe once I'm inside, it will go away.*

She entered the building through the front door and stood for a few seconds in awe. "Wow."

The lobby looked like an expensive hotel with a high ceiling, beautiful fireplace, and paintings on each wall. Large windows formed the front wall looking out onto the lawn and flowerbeds along the sidewalk with yellow and burnt orange chrysanthemums.

"May I help you?" the lady at the front desk asked.

"Yes. I am here to see Eleanor Cook. Could you direct me to her room?"

"And, you are?" the lady asked as she looked at her computer screen over her half-frame glasses.

*How odd to ask that.* "My name is Jaime Wilson. I'm a friend of Eleanor's."

The desk clerk looked to her left. "Lydia," she called. A young nurse's aide approached the desk. "Would you take Ms. Wilson to the Visitation Room?" She turned to Jaime. "I'll have someone bring Mrs. Cook to see you there."

"There's really no need for that. I'd be happy to visit with her in her room," Jaime offered.

"No guests are allowed in the residents' rooms."

"I see. Well, in that case, Lydia, please show me to the Visitation Room."

The young girl led Jaime to a hallway just off from the lobby. Two doors down, they entered a room full of tables and chairs. A few people sat at some tables visiting and at the end of the room, a large-screen television hung on the wall with a couch in front of it.

"You can sit at any of the tables you like," the aide said, and then turned to leave.

"Lydia, could I ask you something?"

"Sure."

"Why can't visitors go to the residents' rooms to visit?"

"It's a security thing and one of the amenities they pay the big bucks for here."

"How much does it cost to live here?"

"I think it's about eight-thousand a month."

"Wow, what does that pay for?" Jaime asked.

"They get the best food, a private room with a big high-definition television, fresh flowers every day, and a personal aide."

Just then, an aide wheeled Eleanor into the room. Jaime took a seat at the table where they parked Eleanor's chair and Lydia left the room.

Jaime thanked the aide who locked the wheels on Eleanor's chair and then took a seat at the same table.

"Could we visit in private?" Jaime asked the aide.

"I'm to stay by Mrs. Cook's side in case she needs something," the aide replied.

"Honey, I'll be fine. You can go," Eleanor requested.

The aide stood to leave, but only went as far as the table by the entrance.

Jaime looked at Eleanor and immediately noticed her wrinkles had deepened; her skin had turned paler, and there was a blank look to her face. She looked as though she had aged several years since Jaime had seen her.

"Eleanor, do you remember me?"

The old woman stared at Jaime for a few seconds. "Jaime."

"Yes. It's good to see you."

"It's good to see you, too."

"I'd like to talk to you alone. Could you ask your attendant to leave?"

Eleanor slowly turned her head toward the attendant." "Gretchen, would you mind leaving us alone?"

"Yes, ma'am." The aide stood and left the room.

When Eleanor turned back to Jaime, she had a totally different look to her face. She appeared more alert with widened eyes.

"I hate having a shadow all the time."

Jaime sat up in surprise by the immediate change.

"They try to keep me drugged up, but I don't really take all the pills. I hide them until I can get to the bathroom and then flush them. I haven't been caught yet." Eleanor winked.

"Oh, Eleanor," Jaime laughed. "You're a smart woman, but how are you really feeling?"

"Well honey, I'm a might stiff most of the time, but that's just my arthritis."

"Do you remember what happened to you? Did you fall?" Jaime asked.

"The only thing I remember was being at home and hearing the kitchen door open and close. I saw Malcolm's car out front through the window, so I thought it was him coming in the house. When he didn't come into the living room, I called his name and walked toward the kitchen. The last thing I remember was my head hurting and I blacked out."

"Malcolm is telling everyone that you had a stroke. Is that a possibility, or could you have tripped and fell, or maybe been hit over the head?"

"I didn't have a stroke. I don't have any paralysis. See." Eleanor moved both of her arms and raised her legs off of the wheelchair's footrests. "The only reason they have me in this chair is because it's such a long walk from my room."

"Eleanor, on the same day that you blacked-out, I was walking out in the woods behind your house and someone pushed me over the edge of the cliff. Ben found me unconscious the next morning. I was in the hospital with a concussion at the same time you were."

"Oh my, and you think someone pushed you?"

"I know someone pushed me." Jaime took a deep breath before continuing. She didn't know how Eleanor would handle the next question. "Do you think Malcolm might have hurt both of us?"

"What? Why on earth would he do such a thing?"

"Ben and I think whoever pushed me doesn't want me investigating the Murdock family disappearance and I think Malcolm might be involved."

"Why?" Eleanor asked.

"He was one of he men who found those Indian bones, but I don't think those bones were ever taken to the university like the newspaper article implied."

Eleanor sat silent and listened.

"Do you remember anything about how Malcolm acted back then?"

Before Eleanor could answer, her attendant walked back in the room. "Mrs. Cook, I'm afraid your visit is over. It's time for you medication and then lunch."

Eleanor winked at Jaime and then went back into her little charade with her frail voice. "Okay, dear."

Jaime gave her hand a squeeze. "Goodbye, Eleanor. I'll come back to visit again soon."

The aide unlocked the wheelchair's wheels and rolled Eleanor out of the room. Lydia had also returned, Jaime assumed to escort her out.

"If you'll come with me, I'll show you back to the lobby."

Neither Jaime nor the young girl spoke they reached the lobby. "Thank you for your assistance, Lydia."

"You're welcome, ma'am. Come again."

"Oh, I plan to." Jaime noticed that as soon as they had entered the lobby, the lady at the front desk didn't take her eyes off of Jaime and Lydia.

Once outside, Jaime decided to take a short cut to the parking lot by going through the facility's garden. Filled with chrysanthemums and other fall flowers, the garden looked bright and full of life.

A few residents milled around. One particular gentleman sat in a wheelchair along the concrete path. As Jaime passed, she smiled at him.

"What are you smiling at?" he sneered in a gruff voice.

She stopped. "Well, it's a beautiful fall day. Isn't that enough to smile about?"

"You kids are all alike. You only look at the surface."

Jaime had dealt with his kind before and knew she couldn't change his mind, so she continued toward the parking lot.

"I saw you talkin' to Eleanor Cook," he called after her.

Again, she stopped and walked back to him, taking seat on the bench next to him. "Yes, I was. How do you know, Eleanor?"

"I used to live near her and her husband."

"Really? I'm Jaime Wilson, from New York City." She extended her hand, which he ignored.

"Name's Jacob Katt."

Jaime remembered Eleanor mentioning that name when they first talked at the library. "Nice to meet you, Mr. Katt."

"What's someone from New York doing visiting Eleanor?"

"Well, I work for a magazine there and I came to Royal to write about the Murdock family disappearance." Katt's eyes widen upon hearing the Murdock name. "Do you remember that happening?"

"I remember. Good riddens to 'em, too."

"You didn't like them?" Jaime wished she had her digital recorder with her.

"That damned Tom Murdock. He..." Katt stopped in mid-sentence and paused. "His cows kept getting' into my cornfield. Hell, if I hadn't kept an eye out, they'd ate up all my profit. And, that wife of his weren't no better."

"It sounds like you didn't like the Murdock's very well."

"Bonnie was the only good one. Had a heart of gold, that girl did."

"Mr. Katt," a male attendant called as he walked toward them. "It's time for lunch."

As the attendant took Katt into the building, Jaime walked to her car and started the drive back to Ben's. Fifteen minutes down the road, her cell phone began ringing. She picked it up and saw Ben's name on the display. "Damn." She turned the radio off hoping he wouldn't hear the highway noises. "Hello."

"Where are you?" His voice was firm and to the point.

"What do you mean, where am I?" *Damn it, he knows.*

"I came home with a few groceries and find you and your car gone. You aren't supposed to be driving yet."

"I drove to Whitely to see Eleanor Cook, and I'm on my way back now. I'm fine, thank you for asking," she responded, sarcastically. "I should be there in about twenty minutes. I learned some things you'll be interested in hearing."

"I'll be waiting for you." The phone line went dead.

"Busted," she said to herself.

After arriving at his house and walking inside, she found him pacing the floor.

"What were you thinking running off to Whitley like that? Something could have happened and caused an accident hurting someone else, or worse, you could have been hurt."

"I'm sorry, but I really needed to see Eleanor."

"It couldn't have waited until tomorrow when I drive you to the doctor. You're worse then a teenager."

"Here. Take these." She held her car keys out to him.

He couldn't help but laugh and Jaime joined in. Ben went to the couch to sit down.

"What did you want to tell me?" he asked.

"It's about Eleanor. They're trying to keep her drugged all the time, but she actually isn't taking the pills. She told me that on the day of her accident, she remembers seeing Malcolm's car in front of her house and hearing someone come in the back door. The next thing she knew her head hurt and she blacked out. Ben, she didn't fall and she didn't have a stroke. Someone hit her over the head."

"Did she say that? Did she say someone hit her?"

"No, not in those words, but she told me she didn't have a stroke. We sort of got off the subject when I told her about my fall."

"There's not much I can do unless she thinks someone hit her."

"I have one more thing." As she continued, she opened her bag by the couch and pulled out a folder full of her research notes and started thumbing through them. "When I left the building, I walked through their garden on the way to the car. I started talking a man in a wheelchair. His name was Jacob Katt. Sound familiar?"

"The only thing I remember about Jacob Katt is that he used to be a very powerful man around here."

Finally, she found what she was looking for in her notes. "Here it is. When I first interviewed Eleanor at the library, she told me about Jacob Katt and Tom Murdock not liking each other. But, that everyone suspected Katt had a love interest in Murdock's daughter, Bonnie. Katt is the perfect suspect."

"I don't remember seeing his name anywhere in the police reports about the disappearance."

"Me either, but when I talked with him today, you should have seen his face when I told him I was researching their disappearance."

"That's interesting."

"He sure didn't like Tom Murdock, but when he talked about Bonnie, his whole demeanor changed. I think Eleanor was right about something going on between them. Can you check into Katt's background and see what you can find?" she asked.

"I will. I need to get back to the office now." He got up and walked to the door with Jaime following. At the door, he turned and looked straight at her, "No more driving until after you see the doctor.

Understand?" He tossed her car keys back to her.

"I understand."

After Ben left, Jaime spent the rest of the afternoon sitting at the kitchen table calling colleges and universities in Indiana looking for Dr. Norman Cabot.

Time had gotten away from her, when suddenly the dog, who had been at her feet all day, jumped up and ran to the living room. Jaime heard the front door open and Ben talking to his dog. She realized it was five-o'clock and she hadn't started anything for dinner.

Ben walked into the kitchen in time to catch her trying to clean up her mess. Notes and clippings were spread all over the table, laptop in front of her, and cell phone plugged into the wall, charging.

"I'm so sorry. I've been working all afternoon and lost track of time. I haven't even started anything for dinner." She then noticed that he held a pizza box in his hands.

"I guess its okay that I forgot to call and tell you I was bringing pizza home then." They both broke into laughter.

"Let me clean off of the table."

"I'll get the plates," he offered.

While she cleared her things, Jaime couldn't help but watch him get the plates and forks. He looked so handsome and sexy in his uniform. The dark brown shirt tailored to fit so nicely over his broad shoulders and muscular arms. Thanks to the warm day, he wore short-sleeves that showed off his taunt biceps. *Is it warm in here, or just me?* she thought.

With her things put aside, they sat down to eat. "I called all the universities in Indiana today with archaeology departments and a couple in northern Kentucky and none of them had ever heard of a Dr. Cabot, or had a record of receiving any skeletons at that time."

"Why does that not surprise me?" He took a bite of his pizza.

"I want to interview Malcolm Cook," she announced.

Ben nearly choked and then began laughing. He took a drink of his beer and swallowed. "You know he won't agree to that."

"I also want to talk to Clayton Spencer and Sam Morgan, too. They were all together when they found the bones and I want to ask them about it."

"I don't think any of them will talk to you. They're the ones that can't wait for you to leave town."

"What if I told them that talking to me could speed up my departure?"

"Wouldn't work. Guarantee it."

"I think it would and I have a plan."

"Of course, you do." Ben closed his eyes and ran his hand down over his face. "Not that I will agree to it, but what's your plan?"

"If we stop and see Eleanor tomorrow after we leave the doctor's office, you could hear what she told me about the day we were both hurt. Then, you would have probable cause to question Malcolm. I could be there too, since I'm a victim."

"You've been watching too many police dramas, but it might work."

"Then, you'll do it? We can also talk to Jacob Katt tomorrow and maybe figure out a way to bring Spencer and Morgan in for questioning, too."

Ben didn't say anything at first. "We'll talk to Eleanor first and maybe Jacob Katt, too. Depending on what they say, I might ask the men to come in, but if they refuse, I can't do anything about it at this time."

"I understand."

They both continued with their dinner.

"I stopped by the library this afternoon and asked Annie about Jacob Katt. I figured she'd know about him and also not blab to the whole county that I was asking."

"What did she say?"

"Katt had a farm near the Murdock's place and he was also big in politics at the time. Off and on for about fifteen years, he was either a County Commissioner or County Councilman and very powerful."

"Really? He doesn't seem like that now. What made him so powerful?"

"From what Annie remembers, his political connections. He approved who got hired and fired from county government jobs and the school system."

"Were people afraid of him and his power?" she asked.

"Back then, the county jobs and school system were about the only local jobs around. If you didn't have one of those jobs and weren't a farmer, you had to drive all they way to Louisville for work."

"Did Annie know if Katt and Bonnie Murdock were seeing each other?"

"She wasn't sure, but did say the best people to ask were the town gossip ladies." Ben took a drink of his beer.

"Annie didn't call them that, did she?"

Ben laughed. "No, she suggested asking the members of the

Women of Royal Club, but it's the same bunch of ladies."

"Isn't that the same club that Helen Morgan asked me to speak at one of their meetings?"

"I think so." He popped the last bite of his pizza into his mouth.

"Maybe I should call and take her up on her offer."

After finishing dinner, Jaime cleared the table and put the dirty dishes in the dishwasher. Satisfied that the kitchen looked clean, she looked up Helen Morgan's phone number and gave her a call.

Afterwards, when Jaime walked into the living room, she found Ben on the couch reading the newspaper. He had changed into jeans and a t-shirt and looked just as sexy in that as he did in his uniform. Jake lay at his feet, sleeping. She sat in the chair and curled her legs under her.

"What time is your doctor's appointment tomorrow?" Ben asked.

"Nine o'clock."

"We should probably leave around eight then."

"Okay. I just got off the phone with Helen Morgan. The Women of Royal Club are having a meeting tomorrow night and I'm now the guest speaker."

"Do you know where she lives? It's pretty far out of town."

"She gave me directions. It didn't sound so hard to find. I'm hoping I can get some more info on Jacob Katt from the ladies."

"Now, how are you going to work that into the discussion?"

"I don't know yet, but I'll figure out some way."

Jaime sat very quiet for several minutes.

Ben lowered the newspaper and folded it, putting it on the table. "Are you okay?"

"I received an email from my editor at the magazine today. I have to be back in New York before the end of next week, whether I'm finished here, or not. She wants my story for the next issue."

"But, you don't have a conclusion yet."

"That's just how I will have to write it and hope it's good enough to get me the assistant editor job."

"It's certainly going to be quiet around here. I've gotten used to coming home to someone everyday," he related.

Ben held his arm out at his side and Jaime moved next to him on the couch. His arm wrapped around her and her head rested on his shoulder.

"Rural life has grown on me. I'm really going to miss being here, too."

The dog got up and moved to Jaime, putting his head on her leg.

# Chapter Twelve

The next morning, Jaime sleepily wandered into the kitchen and found Ben standing over the coffee maker watching the steady stream flow into the pot.

"Does it make it finish quicker when you stare at it?" she asked.

"No, but it makes me happier," he quipped back.

She laughed. "How about a bagel and cream cheese to go with your coffee?"

"Sure, that would be great. I'm sorry, we ran out of decaf coffee."

"That's okay. After I see the doctor today, I'm sure I won't have any restrictions." She sliced through a bagel and popped it in the toaster.

After breakfast, they got in the car and started toward Whitley.

"Are the fall days always this beautiful?" she asked.

"I can't complain. When I lived in Chicago, I really missed seeing all of the colorful trees along the interstate in the fall and the crisp clean air."

"What would you have done if you had lost the election? If you didn't make Sheriff?"

"My property is on the back end of about sixty acres of my family's land. On the other side of those trees behind the house is pasture land where I plant popcorn every year."

"Popcorn?"

"Indiana is one of the biggest popcorn producers in the country."

"So, you would have been a farmer."

"I am a farmer."

"You don't look much like a farmer," she joked. "Ben, I was looking for some dog treats the other day and found a picture of you and Leann. She was beautiful."

"Yes, she was." Silence. "You know, we might see some deer on the drive today. The hunters have them all stirred up in the woods."

Jaime knew the change in subject meant that a discussion about Ben's late girlfriend was off-limits. Neither talked much until they arrived in Whitley.

To their surprise, when they walked into Dr. Summer's waiting room, they found it nearly empty.

"Miss Wilson, you can come back now," the nurse called from the hallway door.

Jaime followed her to an examination room. "Please sit on the exam table." She pulled the electronic thermometer out of its base and after taking Jaime's temperature, she checked her blood pressure and wrote the results on the chart. "Dr. Summers will be in to see you in a few minutes."

"Thank you."

Soon Jaime could hear footsteps coming toward her room and then stopped by the door. Underneath, she could see the doctor's shadow, she assumed, looking through her chart. Finally, the door opened and Dr. Summers walked in.

"Good morning, Miss Wilson."

"Good morning."

"How are you feeling?" he asked.

"I'm feeling very well."

"Good. Let's take a look at you." With his small penlight, he checked each of her eyes. "Are you having any headaches?"

"I had one yesterday, but that's been the only one. I think it was probably because I was out in the bright sunshine. It's didn't last long."

"Follow my finger with your eyes," he instructed, while he moved his forefinger from the right to the left. "Good. Now, let me check your head." The doctor felt around where the bump had been on her head. "Well, young lady, everything looks fine. I think you can resume your normal activities."

"Including driving and drinking caffeine?" she asked.

Dr. Summers laughed. "Yes, even that. Here's a work statement." He filled out the form and signed it.

*Ben will want to see that for sure.* "I really appreciate all you've done."

The doctor handed Jaime the form plus another one and told her to give it to the clerk at the front window. "Good luck, Miss Wilson and stay away from the cliffs."

"I will. Thank you."

After leaving the doctor's office, Jaime and Ben drove to the Whitley Manor Convalescent Center to see Eleanor. As they approached the front desk, Jaime notices a different desk clerk than before.

"May I help you?" the clerk asked.

"Yes, We're here to see Eleanor Cook," Jaime said.

The clerk typed something into her computer. "I'm sorry, but Mrs. Cook has been discharged."

"What? Where did she go?"

"Again, I'm sorry, but privacy laws restrict me from releasing that information."

Jaime turned to Ben, who took out his badge and showed it to the clerk.

"I'm Sheriff Ben Hunter, from Butler County. Mrs. Cook could be a witness to an assault prior to her coming here. I need to know where she is in order to question her."

"One moment, Sheriff." The clerk stepped into an office along the back wall behind the desk. A few minutes later, she returned with another woman accompanying her.

"I'm Catherine Marshall, the Administrator of the facility. I understand you're asking about Eleanor Cook?"

"Yes. Can you tell me where she's moved to?" Ben asked.

"Sheriff, I'm sure you understand that I have to abide by the federal privacy regulations. If you want information on Mrs. Cook, you'll have to bring me a court order."

"I understand. We'd also like to speak with Jacob Katt, if he is still residing here."

"Of course, it's almost lunch time, Mr. Katt can usually be found at the side garden. I can have someone take you there. However, if Mr. Katt does not want to speak with you, you will have to leave the facility."

"That won't be a problem," Ben answered.

Before Ms. Marshall could summon someone, Jaime spoke up. "I know where he is. Thank you." She turned and headed toward the door. Ben nodded to the ladies and followed Jaime out.

"I don't understand. Eleanor didn't say anything yesterday morning about leaving here. Someone must have told Malcolm that I was here speaking to her."

As they entered the garden, Jaime pointed out Katt in the same spot where she found him yesterday."

"Hello, Mr. Katt. I'm Jaime Wilson. Do you remember us talking yesterday?"

"No. I don't remember nothin'. What do you want?" he snapped.

"Do you remember Tom Murdock?" Ben asked.

"That son of a bitch. He wouldn't keep his cows out of my field."

Jaime took a seat on the bench next to Katt's wheelchair and Ben kneeled down to his level.

"Jacob, what about Tom, Judith, and Bonnie?" Ben asked.

Cloudy tears welled in Katt's eyes. "Bonnie, oh my beautiful

Bonnie."

"What happened to Bonnie?" Jaime asked softly as she touched his shoulder.

He began to weep. "She was so sick, so very, very sick."

Jaime changed the subject, "Did you know that Eleanor Cook moved from here yesterday?"

"Yes. I saw her leave yesterday." He wiped the tears from his eyes with his shirt sleeve.

"Do you know where she went?" Ben asked.

"Nope, but I know she didn't want to go."

"How do you know that?"

"Cause I heard her tell Malcolm and he said she had to go."

"Mr. Katt," an attendant called as he approached. "It's time for your lunch." He released the brake on the wheelchair and pushed Katt to the building.

Ben joined Jaime on the bench.

"Katt knows what happened to the Murdock's," Jaime said.

"I believe he does, but he's so confused from dementia, it wouldn't hold up in court."

"Can you question Malcolm now?" she asked.

"I'll talk to him, but it will be unofficial and without you."

"I understand."

* * * *

Later that evening, Jaime came out from her bedroom and walked toward the door. "Wish me luck."

Ben sat on the couch with his socked feet perched upon the coffee table and *Jeopardy* blaring on the television. "You sure you know how to get to Helen Morgan's house? I'd be glad to drive you."

"I have good directions. Don't worry." She put her jacket on and grabbed her bag of notes.

"Call when you start home, okay?"

"I will." She breezed out the door.

The Morgan's lived out in the country on the other side of town. At seven-thirty, the sun had long set and the streetlights of Royal well lit her way through town. Just outside of Royal, she turned right onto a road next to a harvested cornfield. "It should only be a few miles now," she told herself.

Tall, leafless trees now lined both sides of the narrow, curvy road.

"I'd hate to meet a car on this road right now." Finally, she spotted the blue mailbox mentioned in the directions. Turning at the mailbox, and two curves later, she drove up to a two-story colonial home with every window lit brightly.

Outside lights lined the circular driveway. Jaime counted eight cars parked in front and two in the garage.

After parking, she got out and walked to the house. Helen Morgan met her at the door. "Welcome, Jaime. I'm so glad you could make it to our meeting. Please come in."

"Thank you. I'm looking forward to this."

Helen led her into the large living room where twelve ladies were in numerous conversations.

"We've already held our business meeting and have been awaiting your arrival. After your talk, we have coffee and cake waiting for us," Helen explained. "Ladies, ladies, if I could have your attention." The room quieted. "I'd like to introduce our guest speaker, Jaime Wilson."

The ladies applauded and Jaime felt her face warm with a little embarrassment. "Thank you. I'm very honored to be here this evening. I hope I won't disappoint you with my boring life." The ladies laughed.

Jaime proceeded to explain to them about her career as a magazine writer and some of the past stories she had written, ending with why she had come to Royal to research.

"Do you always solve the mysteries you write about?" one lady asked.

"Not always, in fact, most of the time, no."

"What about the story here? Any thoughts on what happened to the Murdock family?" another lady asked.

"I've uncovered some interesting things, but can't really discuss the story before it's published."

"When will that be?"

"I have to have it to my editor next week and it will probably be published in a couple months."

"So, you'll be leaving soon?" a lady asked from the rear of the room.

"Yes, soon and I'll miss it here. I've learned to love country living."

A few of the ladies chuckled at her remark and Jaime knew they were thinking of her relationship with Ben.

"If there are no more questions, I'd love to get to that coffee and cake."

Helen thanked Jaime for coming and then guided everyone to the rear of the house where they could be served. The glassed-in sunroom looked like a conservatory with a rounded roof. Several tables were set with the flatware and lit candles as the centerpieces.

Outside of the glass, hay bales, pumpkins, and cornstalks lined the lit patio. "Helen certainly knows how to decorate," Jaime commented to the lady standing next to her.

"You should see her at Christmas," the lady replied.

A young woman stood to the right, ready to cut and serve the large sheet cake. Another server stood at the other end of the table filling cups with hot coffee.

The guests formed a line, letting Jaime, as the guest of honor, go first. She took a small plate of cake, a cup of coffee, and then sat at the end of one of the tables.

"May I sit with you?" an older lady asked.

"Of course, please, join me," Jaime answered.

"I'm Martha Babcock," the lady said as she sat down.

"I think we've spoken before. At the market in town, I believe."

"Why, yes. I believe you're right. You mentioned something about maybe living here. How is Sheriff Ben?"

*Whoa, straight to the punch.* "He's fine."

"Are you still thinking about living here?"

"Well, that would be difficult since my job is still in New York."

A few other ladies joined them at the table.

"I saw Eleanor Cook the other day. She looked wonderful," Jaime announced. Before anyone could respond, she continued. "I also met Jacob Katt. Now, there's an interesting man."

"Interesting?" Mrs. Babcock laughed.

"Do any of you know him?" Jaime asked.

Several of the ladies nodded yes, but Mrs. Babcock spoke up again. "He never married and other than political or government meetings, he mostly stayed on his farm."

"I heard that he once had a relationship with Bonnie Murdock."

The ladies at the table either looked down at their plate or at each other.

"No one ever saw them in public together, but most everyone suspected they were having relations," Mrs. Babcock said.

"That would have been scandalous back then," another lady added.

"Why is that?" Jaime asked.

"She was probably around twenty years younger than him."

Someone brought up another subject and Jaime took the hint that the discussion of Jacob Katt was finished.

Around ten o'clock, the club members started leaving for their homes and Jaime felt the need to leave, also. Helen walked her to the door.

"Thank you for coming, Jaime. We can't wait to read your story when it comes out."

"I'll make sure the town gets plenty of issues. I really enjoyed meeting everyone tonight."

"Can you find your way back to the highway? I wouldn't want you get lost out here."

"I'm sure I can. Thank you." Jaime got into her car and made her way down the driveway to the narrow road. She checked her cell phone to call Ben as promised, but it showed no signal. "Figures."

The cloudy sky made it seem even darker than when she had arrived earlier. In the rearview mirror, she noticed a set of headlights catching up to her and thought it was one of the stragglers from the meeting.

Soon, they were right on her bumper with their headlights on bright. Finally, when they reached a straight stretch in the road, they started to pass her. Jaime had to hit the brakes to keep from going off the side of the road. As the black truck passes, it blew its horn and sped away.

She had nearly come to a complete stop in the road and pulled out her cell phone again. Having a signal now, she called Ben.

"Ben, I'm on my way back and a truck just about run me off the road."

"What! Where are you?"

"I left Helen's house about five minutes ago, but haven't reached the highway yet."

"I'm on my way," Ben replied.

"No. I'm fine. I'll be there in no time. I'm sure it was probably just some kids impatient with my slow driving."

"I'm going to call the office and have the deputy on duty wait for you in town. She'll follow you to my house to make sure you're okay."

When she drove through, she saw the deputy waiting at the main intersection. The female deputy gave her a wave and pulled out behind her. At the road where Ben lived, Jaime made the turn and the deputy followed.

Twenty minutes later, when Jaime turned into Ben's driveway, the deputy did the same, but stopped and back the car back out, flipped the red lights on and off and drove away.

She saw Ben waiting on the porch. "What happened?" he asked when she reached him.

"I'm sure it was nothing. I was driving slowly and they were probably eager to get by me. The road was so narrow that I thought I was going to end up in the ditch."

"I knew I should have driven you."

"Ben, you can't babysit me the whole time I'm here. I'm really tired and want to go to bed."

She went inside the house and to her room. She wanted to makes some notes from the things the ladies said at the meeting tonight. The night had taken a toll on her and it didn't take long before she crawled into bed and fell asleep.

* * * *

The next morning, Jaime walked into the kitchen finding a pot of coffee already made and a note in front of it from Ben. She poured herself a cup and read the note.

*I have to work through the dance tonight, so I won't be home until late. I hope to see you there.*

*Ben*

She took her coffee to the living room and turned on a news channel on the television. She sat on the couch and began reading *The Messenger-News* that Ben had left on the table. As she looked through the pages, she admired how the newspaper's staff had managed not to miss publishing a single issue of the weekly periodical since the fire. While sitting there, her cell phone rang.

"Hello."

"Hey, sweetie."

"Gabby! It's so good to hear your voice."

"How are you and how is that gorgeous sheriff?" Gabby asked.

"I'm fine, and so is Ben."

"Jaime, when are you coming back to the city? Charlotte wants you back in the office."

"I was planning on coming back next week, but was going to drive back and go through Pennsylvania to research an Amish story first."

"You can't. Charlotte wants both you and your story here by the end of the day on Monday."

"I really hoped for some time to myself before coming back to the office."

"So, how are things with Ben?"

"I'm trying my best to not fall for him, but it's hard when he wants a relationship. I love my career and miss the city, but rural life has grown on me."

"You're going to have to make your decision soon."

"You're right. I'll decide today and tell him after the Halloween dance tonight."

"Oh my gosh, is that tonight? I wish I were there to go with you. What's your costume?"

"Costume? I was just going to wear a sweater and jeans."

"You have to try and come up with something and I want pictures."

Jaime laughed. "I'll try. Thanks for calling, Gabby. I needed to hear your voice. I'll call you tomorrow and let you know what I decide."

After hanging up her phone, she picked up her laptop and checked her email. Sure enough, there was an email from Charlotte Miller, editor of the magazine, telling Jaime she wanted her back at the office.

She closed her email and began typing out the rest of her story. Once finished, she typed out an emailed to the editor, attached the story, and hit send. "I hope I made the right decision," she said aloud.

Later that night, Jaime pulled in and parked her car at the Royal Community Center where the Halloween Dance was being held. Ben's police car sat by the front door.

Once inside, the large room had been decorated like a barn. Lots of hay bales had been placed along one wall, with wooden cutouts of cows, pigs, and horses. She looked around the room for Ben. One side of the room had tables and chairs full of people enjoying refreshments.

Since he was on duty, she didn't think he would be with the people in the middle of the room dancing to the music of the country band on the stage. Finally, she spotted him walking toward her

"Wow, I love your police costume. It looks so real," she teased.

"Don't think I haven't heard that about a hundred times tonight. I wish it were a costume because I'd like to take you out on the dance floor." He took a deep breath. "But, since I'm working, I probably shouldn't." He stepped back to look at her costume. "Very nice, an Indiana University basketball player's warm-up suit, complete with striped pants."

"I really had to think hard to come up with a costume. I almost wore one of your uniform shirts, but didn't want to add impersonating an office to my list of charges since arriving. I got this when Gabby and I were at the university looking for Dr. Cabot."

A few people walked by to say hello to Ben. Jaime guessed they wanted to get a better look at her, since she had become quite the topic of gossip after moving into Ben's home.

"Would you like some punch?" he asked.

"That would be really good. It's kind of warm in here."

"Why don't you go and sit on the bleachers over there and I'll bring some to you."

Jaime saw Deputy Stokes standing at the end of the bleachers. She walked over and sat down by him. "Hello, Mark. How are you this evening?" she asked.

"I'm just fine, ma'am."

"Ma'am? There's no need to be so formal. It's Jaime, remember."

"I'll try and remember."

Ben approached and handed Jaime a cup of punch and then sat down next to her.

"I better go make a round through the parking lot. Lots of opportunities for mischief tonight," Stokes said.

"See you later, Mark." Jaime took a drink of punch.

"Yes ma-," he started to say and then catching himself. His face blushed red and he turned and headed outside.

When the band took a break, Martha Babcock stood on the stage speaking into the microphone. "Would all of the children who are in costume please come up on stage? It's time for the costume contest."

"I remember being a kid in that contest," Ben stated.

"Really? How were you dressed?"

"I was a wild west sheriff, complete with six-shooters."

"The outfit hasn't changed much, has it?"

"I guess not." He laughed.

"Did your costume win?"

"I lost to a kid dressed as a clown. I haven't liked clowns since."

With the children now on the stage and the lights dimmed, she felt Ben take her hand into his. She looked at him and found him smiling back as he gave her hand a squeeze.

When the spark from his touch reached her heart, her chest became tight and she couldn't get her breath. I have to get out of here." She jumped off the bleachers and ran outside.

Ben followed and caught up with her at her car. "I'm sorry." He turned her around. "What's wrong? Why are you crying?"

"I have to go. I can't talk now, not here. She tried to open her car door, but Ben blocked her.

"I'm not letting you leave like this. What's wrong?"

He wiped a tear from her cheek. "I really do need to talk to you, but not here in the parking lot."

"I have to work until midnight," he told her.

"I'll wait up for you."

"Okay. You're sure you're okay to drive?"

"I'm fine."

He stepped aside and opened the car door for her. "Be careful and I'll be home as soon as I can."

Jaime got in the car and drove out of the parking lot heading back to Ben's. Driving through the deserted town gave her an eerie feeling. "Everyone from town must be at the dance," she commented to herself.

About a half-mile outside of town, a set of headlights started following her. She frantically watched in the rearview mirror as they now looked to be only feet from her bumper. Thoughts from the night before flashed through her mind. Just as she reached for her cell phone, the truck rammed her bumper. The car jerked and her cell phone went flying, landing on the floor of the passenger side.

Her grip on the steering wheel tightened with each hit. The truck now made constant contact and pushed her car off of the road into a deep ditch. The car jolted to a stop and the air bag deployed with a loud bang. Then, silence.

Through the broken side window, she saw the black truck had stopped and someone was walking toward her wearing a Halloween mask of a vampire. Her cell phone, nowhere to be seen.

"Go back to New York, or your next accident will be your last." The man turned and ran back to the truck and sped off.

Jaime slowly moved each limb to make sure they worked without pain. *No broken bones, I think. That's good.* She released her seatbelt and tried to open her door, but it wouldn't budge. Then, she heard it. A car approached. She pushed harder against the door, fearing her attacker had decided to return.

Instead, a teenage couple got out of a car and ran to help.

"Ma'am, are you okay?" the boy asked.

"Yes. Please help me out of here."

"You shouldn't move." He turned to his girlfriend. "Call 9-1-1."

"Will you help me out of this car?" Jaime shouted.

"Yes, ma'am." The boy tugged on the door until it finally opened and he helped her out of the car.

Several minutes later, the ambulance pulled up with Deputy Stokes and the fire department following.

The paramedics helped Jaime, who protested the whole time, to the ambulance.

Stokes stood at the back door of the ambulance while Jaime was being checked over. "Jaime, what happened?"

"Someone ran me off the road." She turned to the paramedic trying to take her blood pressure," Will you stop that? I told you, I'm fine."

"What kind of vehicle was it?" Stokes asked.

"Officer, can you wait until we're finished?" the medic asked.

Stokes nodded and pulled out his cell phone as he stepped back from the door.

"I keep telling you, I'm not hurt," she repeated.

"Miss Wilson, please let me decide that."

Jaime finally laid back on the stretcher and let him do his work. Just as they were finished, she heard a siren in the distance getting louder as it approached. With the back door of the ambulance still open, she saw Ben screech to a stop. He jumped out of his car, red and blue lights still flashing, and rushed to the ambulance.

"Sheriff," the paramedic greeted him.

"Dan," he returned the greeting. "How's the patient?"

"I'm right here and conscious and I'm fine."

Ignoring her, the paramedic answered, "I think she's fine, but should get checked out at the hospital to be sure."

"Mind if I speak to her alone, to take her statement?"

The medic stepped out of the ambulance. Ben got in and sat next to Jaime. Again, he took her hand into his. "What happened?"

"A black truck ran me off the road."

"Did it look like the same truck as last night?"

"It could have been, but there's more. After he ran me off the road, he stopped and walked over to me. He said if I didn't go back to New York, the next accident would be my last." She felt Ben's hand tense around hers.

"You saw him? What did he look like?"

"He wore a Halloween mask."

"Okay. I'll follow you to the hospital. After they check you out, I'll bring you home."

"I don't need to go to the hospital. There's nothing wrong with me," she insisted.

"Sheriff," the paramedic interrupted. "We should go."

Ben looked at Jaime. "Go to the hospital."

"Fine."

He released her hand and got out. "Dan, I'm going to follow you to the hospital. She said the guy that ran her off the road threatened her afterward."

"Thanks, Sheriff. We appreciate the escort."

"Stokes, put an alert out on a black pickup with damage to the front end; approach with caution. The driver threatened her."

The paramedic closed the ambulance door and they headed for the hospital.

When Ben and Jaime later returned to Ben's home, the clock on the wall showed two o'clock. "You're sure you're okay?" he asked.

"For the hundredth time, I am fine and you heard the ER doctor say that, too."

"We'll find the person who did this. I will keep you safe. I promise."

"Ben, remember at the dance when I said we needed to discuss something? I think we need to do that now." She paced back and forth behind the big chair.

"You've had kind of a rough night. Can't it wait until morning?" he suggested.

She stopped her pacing. "That's just it, it can't wait until morning. It can't wait any longer."

"Okay, let's sit down and talk." He touched her elbow.

She threw up her arm. "I can't sit down."

"Jaime, what is going on?"

She looked over at him; stared into his eyes and saw his fatigue. "I finished my story today and emailed it to my editor. I'm flying back to New York tomorrow."

Ben hesitated before speaking. "Is that what you want to do?"

"Yes, it's what's best for me." Wiping her eyes, she started pacing again. "You don't know how I struggled with this decision." She stopped, took a deep breath, and looked at him. "My editor told me the assistant editor job was mine, as long as I'm back at the office by Monday morning."

"I don't know what to say."

"For years I worked so hard so I could have the experience and credentials to be a magazine editor. I had to do it."

"I understand. I don't like it, but I understand."

As if they knew each other's thoughts, he opened his arms and she walked into them as he wrapped them around her.

"We still have a few hours before morning."

Before she could answer, he picked her up and carried her to his bedroom, kicking the door closed behind them.

* * * *

The next morning, the long ride to the airport lacked it usual conversation. "We'll stop by the rental company counter at the airport so I can drop off the accident report," Ben said.

"Okay."

After arriving at the airport and taking care of the rental car accident report, the time came to say goodbye. They stood at the entrance to the Security Gate.

"I'll email you the final copy of my article once the editor finishes it."

"I'll keep you updated on that black truck and if I find anything more about what happened to the Murdock family."

"Good."

"I'm going to officially question Malcolm Cook, Clayton Spencer, and Sam Morgan, too."

"Make sure you call and tell me about it." Tears swelled in her eyes and his glistened. She could see he fought hard to hold back his emotions. "I better go. Please tell everyone goodbye for me."

Ben took her into his arms for what seems like the longest hug she'd ever had. She broke away first.

"Goodbye." Turning, she fell in line with the other people going through the checkpoint.

Once through the metal detector, she grabbed her bag from the conveyor belt, and turned to take one last look at her handsome sheriff. She gave him a wave and did her best to smile. He did the same. She turned and walked away from the checkpoint, fighting the urge to turn and run back into his arms.

# Chapter Thirteen

*Six weeks later*

Jaime and Gabby, with coffee in hand, sat at a table in Starbucks just around the corner from their office in Manhattan.

"I can't believe we actually got a table for a change," Gabby said.

"Must be the rainy weather's sending everyone straight home after work," Jaime replied.

"It's been a long week. I'm so glad it's Friday." Gabby took a drink of her Skinny Caramel Macchiato.

"Me, too. This coffee is just what I needed. I love this Peppermint Mocha Latte." She took a sip of her drink.

"Heard from Ben lately?"

"Only one short phone call this week. When I first got back to town, we emailed or talked over the phone almost every day, but they're becoming less and less often now. He wants me to come visit, but this new assistant editor job is keeping so busy, I take work home with me every weekend."

"Why can't he come here to see you?" Gabby asked.

"He says he wants to, but can't get away from his job either."

"If this relationship is going to work, one or both of you are going to have to compromise." Gabby looked at her watch. "Oh my gosh, it's almost six o'clock. I have to get home and ready for a date." She stood up to leave.

"I better get home, too. Of course, there's nothing for me tonight except work."

"Sweetie, call Ben and work something out with him." She leaned closer to Jaime. "You need some sex with that man. It cures whatever ails you."

Jaime laughed. The ladies picked up their coffees and headed out the door. Both opened their umbrellas in the steady rain.

"See you, Monday."

"Have a good weekend," Jaime called back after her. She flagged down a taxi. On the ride home, she thought about Ben. It had been weeks since she they had seen each other and she longed for his warm, comforting hugs.

Once home at her apartment, Jaime took a quick shower and donned some sweatpants and a long-sleeved Giants t-shirt. She popped a frozen dinner to cook in the microwave and ate it while checking her e-mail. Nothing from Ben.

Finally, as she listened to the downpour of rain hitting her balcony, she poured herself a glass of wine and sat on the couch to work on editing an article for the magazine. Around nine p.m., *ding-dong*. The sound startled her. She got up and looked through the peephole. "Oh my gosh." She unlocked the door and opened it to a very wet Ben Hunter.

"What are you doing here?" she asked as she started to rush into his arms.

Ben put his arms out stopping her from touching him. "I'm soaked, don't hug me yet."

"I don't care." She tried her best to get to him, but he had a firm hold on her shoulders. She couldn't help but laugh.

"Show me where I can change into some dry clothes and then I'll be ready for a proper welcome."

Jaime showed him to the bathroom. "Put you wet clothes in the bathtub and I'll wash them tomorrow for you. There are towels in the closet."

"Will do," he called from the other side of the door.

"You sure you don't need some help in there?"

"I can manage."

"Yeah, but I can't. Would you like some wine?"

"That sounds great."

While he finished changing, she went to the kitchen and poured another glass of wine and also sliced some cheese to go with it. Just as she sat the tray on the coffee table in the living room, Ben appeared.

"Now?" she asked.

"Now."

He opened his arms and she ran into his embrace. She couldn't remember a hug ever feeling so good. When she looked up at him, their lips met. Those sweet lips that she last touched six weeks ago at the airport felt so right.

"You're cold. Come, your wine is on the table."

She cleared her paperwork off the couch and they sat down. He took a drink of his wine and she sat with her head on his shoulder.

"Why didn't you tell me you were coming? I could have picked you up at the airport."

"It was a last minute decision. Mark told me he would work this weekend, if I wanted to come see you." He took another drink of his wine. "I think everyone at the department was glad I came. They had started calling me Grumpy."

"Have I got a cure for you." She remembered what Gabby suggested about sex curing what ailed you. "I know it's raining, but how did you get so wet going from the taxi into my building?"

"There was a traffic jam and I didn't want to wait. I walked the last five blocks. I can't believe the clothes in my bag stayed dry."

"Wet or not, I'm glad you're here." She stretched up and gave him a kiss.

He reached for a slice of cheese and took a bite. "I had another reason for coming to see you. I wanted to update you on the Murdock case."

"Really? You discovered something?"

"I convinced the judge to issue a court order to exhume the skeletons from the graves on the Cook farm."

"What did you find?" She put a piece of cheese on a cracker and popped it into her mouth.

"Three skeletons and I sent them to the State Medical Examiner, who determined that they were the Murdock family."

"How did they identify them?" she asked.

"When the graves were dug up, there were jewelry and other items found in the pockets of clothing. They were used to identify them."

"I knew those weren't Indian graves."

"Once we knew who the skeletons were, that gave me probably cause to question Clayton Spencer, Sam Morgan, and Malcolm Cook. They confessed."

Jaime sat up quickly. "They killed the family?"

"No. They only confessed to getting rid of the bodies, but didn't tell who killed them."

"Well, who did it?"

"Jacob Katt killed Tom and Judith."

"I knew it." She slapped her knee. "What about the daughter? Who killed Bonnie?"

"Remember when we talked with Katt at the nursing home? He said something about Bonnie being sick."

"I remember."

"Katt had gone to the Murdock's home to see Bonnie. When he got there, he found her very sick with pneumonia. He wanted to go for the doctor, but Tom Murdock would hear of it."

"Why wouldn't he want the doctor to come?" Jaime asked.

"The Murdock's didn't have much money and couldn't pay for the doctor." Ben took a drink of his wine. "Katt told him he'd pay and would take her to the doctor himself."

"He really did love her, didn't he?"

"Murdock didn't like Katt's relationship with his daughter, so he tried to stop him and that's when they fought."

"They physically fought?"

"Yes. Judith Murdock had been tending to her daughter and came out from the bedroom and found the two men fighting. She tried to get between them, but was pushed away. She fell and hit her head on the fireplace. She died right there."

"That's terrible."

"When Tom realized she was dead, it infuriated him even more and he went after Katt again. Katt grabbed a knife off of the table and had to kill Tom in self-defense."

"But, how did Bonnie die?"

"After the fight, he went to Bonnie and found that she was far worse then he thought. He knew her end was near, so he sat with her until she died that evening."

"That's so sad. If they would have just let Katt take her to the doctor, Bonnie might have lived and her parents wouldn't have suffered such a horrible death."

"Exactly right," Ben replied, and then continued the story. "The next day, Katt buried all three bodies in the woods."

"I thought you said the three men buried the bodies."

"That happened a few years later. Katt often visited Bonnie's grave and after one rainy spring, Katt found the dirt was washing away from the graves, revealing some of the bones. That's when he coerced the men into reburying the bones near the Cook Farm. Remember, Katt was a powerful man in the county and he promised each man a county job if they helped and kept their mouth shut about it."

"That's some story. Did you arrest them all?" she asked.

"I arrested Clayton Spencer, Sam Morgan, and Malcolm Cook for tampering with evidence and Katt for manslaughter. Katt already pled guilty and has been sent to a state prison with a good medical facility. He'll spend the rest of this life there."

"What about the black truck that ran me off the road?"

"The three men admitted that they hired someone from Whitley to do it. As soon as they knew why you had come to Royal, they started planning on how to scare you back to the city. So, the mystery of the missing Murdock family is solved, thanks to you." He leaned over and kissed her.

"I'm glad I could help, but I have another question. Who pushed me over the cliff?"

"Oh, that was Malcolm and he also assaulted his mother. He thought she knew you were back there and he didn't want to leave any witnesses."

"He tried to kill his own mother?"

"Malcolm said he only wanted to hurt her enough for her to have to go into a nursing home."

"Poor Eleanor, to have your own son hurt you like that."

"She was none to happy to learn about it, but she still hired the best lawyer around to represent Malcolm."

"I'll be glad to testify, if it goes to a trial."

"I knew you would." Ben squeezed her closer with his arm. "I miss you, Jaime."

"I miss you, too."

"How is your new job?"

"It's great; exactly what I dreamed of, even though the work is never done." She gestured to the pile of papers on the coffee table.

"I'm glad you're happy with it."

Jaime saw what she believed to be disappointment in his eyes. "Really?"

"No. I was hoping you'd say you hated it so I could talk you into coming back to Indiana with me."

"Ben, I..."

"You still could do that."

"Do what?"

"You could come live with me. The house is so quiet and lonely without you."

If this conversation continued, she knew she would burst into tears. "Let's not talk about that now. How long can you stay in New York?" she asked.

"I have a return flight on Sunday."

"We don't want to waste a minute longer then." Jaime took Ben's hand and led him to her bedroom.

* * * *

*Monday - Noon*

"I'll have the Red Leaf Salad with Chardonnay Vinaigrette and Raspberry Tea," Gabby told the waitress.

"And, I'll have the Strawberry Salad with the Strawberry Vinaigrette and regular ice tea, no lemon," Jaime said.

"Thank you." The waitress took their orders to the kitchen.

"Ben wants me to move to Indiana," Jaime blurted out.

"Are you going?" Gabby asked.

Jaime hesitated before answering. "No. I couldn't do that. If I hadn't got that promotion, I might consider it, but I couldn't possibly leave my job now."

"You might want to consider it. Who knows if you'll ever find another man like Ben who loves you so much."

Gabby wasn't making it any easier. *What if she were right?* "How do you know I won't find another man? It's a big city with thousands of eligible bachelors out there."

"Do you love Ben?"

"I think I do."

"Then why are you even talking about other eligible bachelors?"

Gabby made very good sense.

\* \* \* \*

*Five Weeks Later*

Ben sat at his desk with Mark Stokes while two other deputies sat in front listening to him and Stokes fill them in on the day's activities as they did every weekday evening at five-o'clock.

"Can you think of anything else?" Ben asked Stokes.

"No, you covered it all."

"Well, I think it's time for me to head home. Gentlemen, have a good weekend."

The deputies left the room leaving Ben and Stokes alone.

"Do you have any plans for dinner on Sunday?" Stokes asked.

"Football, ham sandwiches, and sleeping, not necessarily in that order."

"I'll be going to my mom and dad's and Mom told me to ask you over for dinner."

"That's nice of your mom, and I appreciate it, but I think I'll stay home. Tell her I said thanks."

"Okay. If you change your mind, dinner will be around four-o'clock."

After saying goodnight to everyone at the office, Ben and Stokes walked outside; Ben to his patrol car and Stokes to his truck. "Looks like we're in for a little snow," Stokes said.

"Yeah, hopefully the roads won't get too slick."

"Have a good weekend, boss."

"You, too." Ben got into his car and headed home. With daylight coming to an end and an overcast sky, it was nearly dark by the time he arrived home.

Immediately, he noticed the living room light through the front window as he turned into his driveway. *I thought I turned that off this morning.*

He stepped onto the porch and found the front door unlocked. *Now I know I didn't do that.* He took his gun out of the holster and slowly stepped inside. Ben listened for any noise and heard nothing, but he did notice a light coming from the back of the hallway. Then, he realized that Jake did not come to greet him. *He always hears my car and is waiting inside the door to go out.*

As slowly as he dared, Ben crept down the hall one step at a time until he reached the doorway to the kitchen. There in front of the stove, stood Jaime, stirring a pot on the stove with Jake lying at her feet.

Ben put his gun back in the holster and stepped into the kitchen. When Jaime saw him, she ran into his arms.

"What are you doing here?" he asked between kisses.

I wanted to surprise you and I have some news to share, but before I do, you should go clean up for dinner and I'll finish making the potato soup."

Ben obliged as she rushed him out of the kitchen. Twenty minutes later when he stepped out of the bedroom, the aroma of fresh baked bread filled the air. He followed the scent back to the kitchen.

"Perfect timing," Jaime said and led him to the table to sit. "Would you like something to drink?"

"Sure, a beer would be good. Did you bake bread?"

"Not exactly. I found some bread dough in your freezer from when I was here in October and baked it. Smells great, doesn't it?"

"Sure does."

She ladled some soup into both of their bowls and brought the bread from the oven.

"This is going to be a good weekend after all. Now, tell me your big news."

Jaime put her spoon down and took a drink of wine. "I was hoping that your offer of me moving in was still good."

"Why?" he suspiciously inquired.

"I've been so miserable since you left. I don't want to feel that way anymore. So, if you'll still have me, I'd like to move in, permanently."

"What about your job, and your apartment?"

"I've taken a week off and I can email my two-week notice tomorrow. But, it may take me more than two weeks to move out of my apartment. So, do you still want me?" she asked.

Ben didn't answer. Instead, he stood up and walked out of the room. Jaime became confused and just a little worried. Finally, he came back in. "I had hoped to do this two weeks ago at your apartment, but when you mentioned how much you loved your job, I just couldn't do it. Now I can."

Ben knelt down on one knee in front of her and took her left hand into his. "Jaime, I love you. Will you marry me?" He slipped a diamond ring on her finger.

"Yes, yes, yes!" she exclaimed.

Ben stood and swept her into his arm.

"I love you, Ben Hunter."

"I've loved you since the first moment I saw you at the library," he answered.

As they hugged and kissed, the first snowflakes began to fall.

## *THE END*

# ABOUT THE AUTHOR

Carol Preflatish lives in southern Indiana and shares a log cabin with her husband and two cats in what seems like an enchanted forest with a menagerie of wildlife constantly visiting. Her interest in writing began in high school when she worked as a reporter, photographer, and Sport's Editor for the school newspaper. She is currently the author of five novels and two non-fiction books. Carol enjoys writing romantic suspense and is a member of the Sisters in Crime organization and Kentuckiana Authors.

You can learn more about Carol by visiting her web pages at:
http://CarolPre.webs.com
http://www.facebook.com/AuthorCarolPreflatish

www.ingramcontent.com/pod-product-compliance
Lightning Source LLC
Chambersburg PA
CBHW021110130626
46554CB00002B/617